DOCTOR WHO
DEADLY ASSASSIN

DOCTOR WHO
AND THE
DEADLY ASSASSIN

Based on the BBC television serial *The Deadly Assassin*
by Robert Holmes by arrangement with the British
Broadcasting Corporation

TERRANCE DICKS

published by
the Paperback Division of
W. H. Allen & Co. Ltd.

A Target Book
Published in 1977
by Wyndham Publications Ltd
A Howard & Wyndham Company
44 Hill Street, London W1X 8LB

Second impression 1980

Text of book copyright © 1977 by Terrance Dicks
and Robert Holmes

'Doctor Who' series copyright © 1977 by the
British Broadcasting Corporation
Printed in Great Britain by
Richard Clay (The Chaucer Press) Ltd,
Bungay, Suffolk

ISBN 0 426 11965 7

Contents

1

Vision of Death

The telescopic-sight moved slowly across the crowded hall. The glowing dot of light in the middle of the view-finder paused, hovered, centred on an ornately-robed figure in the middle of the central platform. A finger tightened steadily on the trigger ... There was the fierce crackle of a staser-bolt ... The President jerked and crumpled to the floor ...

'No,' shouted the Doctor. 'No!' He stood in the centre of the TARDIS control-room, hands gripping the edge of the control console. So vivid had been the sudden hallucination that it took him a moment to realise where he really was. The Doctor shook his head dazedly, running long fingers through a tangle of curly hair. 'First the summons to the Panopticon,' he muttered. And now this ... What's *happening* to me?'

It had all started at the end of yet another adventure with Sarah Jane Smith, his young companion. They were safely back in the TARDIS, about to return to Earth, when the Doctor heard a deep, booming gong-note echoing through his mind. It was a call no Time Lord could ever ignore—the summons to the Panopticon. Returning the TARDIS to Earth, the Doctor said a hurried farewell to Sarah, almost bundling her from the control room. He realised she was more than a little hurt that their long friendship was being broken off so abruptly. But the Time Lord summons took precedence over everything else.

Once Sarah had been returned to Earth again the Doctor put the TARDIS on course for his home planet. Now, with Gallifrey very close, this sudden vision of assassination flashed into his mind ...

As he re-checked the instruments the Doctor's mind drifted back over the past. He remembered his youth on Gallifrey, the long years of training to fit him for the place on the High Council that seemed his unavoidable destiny. He remembered the steadily growing build-up of anger and frustration in his own mind at the never-ending ceremonials and elaborately costumed rituals, the endless accumulation of second-hand knowledge that would never be used. A final crisis had provoked rebellion. He had 'borrowed' the TARDIS and fled through Time and Space, determined to see the Universe for himself. After many adventures there had come capture, exile to Earth, and at last freedom again—his reward for dealing with the terrible Omega crisis. Now he was on his way back to Gallifrey, a planet to which he had once sworn never to return. Returning because, after all the long years of rebellion, at heart he was still a Time Lord!

The Doctor smiled wryly at the contradictions in his own nature—*and suddenly he was in the Panopticon again, forcing his way through the packed crowd, thrusting aside the robed figures that obstructed his path. A fleeting glimpse of astonished, shouting faces, and he broke away from the clutch of*

8

restraining hands ...

Now he was high up in one of the encircling galleries, the President's robed figure tiny on the platform below. Powerlessly he felt his own finger tightening on the trigger. There was the crackle of a staser-blast ... The President fell ...

... and so did the Doctor, rolling over as he hit the floor of the TARDIS. He struggled to his feet, and went to the console. The centre column had stopped moving. He was back on Gallifrey.

The approach of the TARDIS had been registered on one of the most advanced security scanning systems in the Galaxy. Now a metallic voice was echoing through the areas of tunnels and walk-ways known as the Cloisters, which connected the towers of the Capitol. 'Sector Seven alert. Unauthorised capsule entry imminent. Chancellery Guard stand to in Sector Seven.'

It reflects great credit on the Guard that they responded promptly and efficiently to this call. There were very few emergencies on Gallifrey, least of all within the Capitol, that impressive complex of Government buildings from which the Time Lord planet was administered. Usually the Guard's only function was to add colour and dignity to ceremonial occasions. Nevertheless, within minutes of the call they came pounding into the still empty Cloisters, spreading out in an armed cordon.

They waited tensely, keen alert young soldiers, hand-picked from the oldest families on Gallifrey.

Service in the Chancellery Guard was a keenly sought honour. A strange, wheezing, groaning sound shattered the silence, and a battered blue box appeared beneath one of the arches. Was this the dangerous intruder? Hands clutching their staser-guns in unaccustomed excitement, they waited for orders.

The Doctor studied the scanner, recognising his surroundings immediately. 'Right in the Capitol itself! They're not going to like *that*.' He adjusted the vision-field to take in the cordon of armed Guards. They looked dangerously keyed-up, capable of shooting him the moment he popped his head out. 'Now I'm in trouble. What a welcome! Surrounded by big-booted soldiers, the minute I get home.'

With impressive dignity, two officers made their way through the cordon, and marched up to the TARDIS. Senior in both age and rank was Castellan Spandrell, Commander of the Chancellery Guard, responsible for all security within the Capitol. He was a man of medium height, unusually broad and muscular for a Time Lord, with a heavy, impassive face that disguised a keen intelligence. Spandrell was a tough, sardonic character, made cynical by long years in Security. He had seen too much of the underside of Time Lord life to have any illusions about it, and his blunt no-nonsense manner had upset many a self-important Government official. Spandrell survived because of his integrity and his efficiency. No one else could cope with his difficult and thankless job. Beside Spandrell stood Commander Hildred, young, eager, and desperately keen to distinguish himself, overjoyed that the emergency had happened in *his* sector.

Hildred ran all round the TARDIS, like a terrier on the scent, and came back to Spandrell. 'You know, Castellan, if I didn't know better, I'd swear this was a Type Forty time capsule.'

Spandrell nodded. 'It is.' He looked at the TARDIS almost affectionately. He'd used a Type Forty himself in the old days. He thumped the side of the police box with a massive fist. 'Chameleon circuit appears to be stuck, though. Still, it's a wonder the thing's still in one piece.'

Hildred was staring wonderingly at the TARDIS. 'But it's impossible, Commander. There are no more Type Forties in service. They're out of commission—obsolete.'

The Doctor gave the TARDIS console a consoling pat. 'Obsolete? Twaddle. Take no notice, old thing!'

Spandrell's face filled the scanner-screen, and his voice boomed over the audio circuits. 'Nevertheless, Commander Hildred, this *is* a Type Forty TARDIS and it's landed in an unauthorised zone just before a very important ceremony. I want the occupants arrested.'

The Doctor sighed.

Spandrell stepped back to take a better look at the TARDIS. 'Now, as I remember, the barrier on this model is a single-curtain trimonic. You'll need a cypher-indent key to get in.'

Hildred came to attention, clicking his heels. 'Very

good, Castellan. I'll send for one at once.'

Spandrell looked thoughtfully at him. He was reluctant to leave matters to Hildred, who was both over-eager and inexperienced, but at this particular time there were many other duties claiming his attention. Still, if he left full instructions ... 'After you've arrested the occupants, put them in safe custody, and impound the machine.' Surely that covered everything, thought Spandrell. Even Hildred couldn't go wrong with such a simple task.

Hildred saluted. 'Very good, Castellan. Will you want to question the prisoners?'

'Eventually, Hildred, eventually. But *not* on Presidential Resignation day.' Spandrell moved away.

Inside the TARDIS, the Castellan's last words were echoing in the Doctor's mind. 'Presidential Resignation Day ...' *The hovering rifle-shot settled on its target. The President crumpled and fell ...* Hallucination—or premonition? The Doctor looked at the scanner screen, and the encircling Guards. If he came out now he'd be thrown into a cell and forgotten until the Ceremony was over. Somehow he had to get past those Guards, and warn the President ...

Castellan Spandrell made his way to the Archive Tower, home of the Capitol's Records Section. The Tower was actually one enormous computer, and as he entered the readout room, Spandrell was impressed, as always, by the air of timeless calm that filled this part of the Capitol complex. All around him data banks quietly hummed and throbbed, while soft-footed Recorders moved unhurriedly to and fro. As Spandrell entered, Co-ordinator Engin bustled forward to greet him. Engin was old, even for a Time Lord, not only in the number of his regenerations but in the physical age of his present body. He had spent all of his lives in the Records Section, beginning as a humble data Recorder, rising slowly through the centuries to his present eminence. Engin's present body was almost worn-out now, and he was bent and shrunken with age, his hair snowy-white, his face wrinkled like an old apple. His next and probably final regeneration was long overdue. But Engin constantly refused to take the time away from his duties, insisting that since he never left the computer area anyway, his present body would serve for a year or two yet.

Despite his great age, Engin was still brisk and efficient, and his eyes were alive with curiosity. 'This is a great honour, Castellan. How may I be of service to you?'

Spandrell replied with equal formality. 'Just a little information, Co-ordinator. If I could have a terminal?'

Engin ushered him to a secluded booth, made a quite unnecessary check on the terminal controls, then busied himself with the study of a data bank—not quite out of earshot.

Spandrell touched a control in front of him. 'Data retrieval. Request information on all Type Forty time travel capsules currently operational.'

There was a moment's silence, then the calm,

emotional computer voice said, 'Negative information. Type Forty capsules are all de-registered and non-operational.'

Spandrell considered. Computers, even Time Lord computers, didn't really think. They could usually tell you what you asked, but they never volunteered information, never saw through to the reasons behind your question. A computer was a kind of idiot genius. You had to make all your questions very clear, because the computer would tell you exactly what you asked —and nothing more.

Carefully he formulated his next request. 'Report number of de-registrations.'

'Three hundred and four.'

'Report original number of registrations.'

'Three hundred and five.'

Impatiently Spandrell snapped, 'Report reason for numerical imbalance.' Under his breath he added, 'You stupid great tin box.'

'One capsule removed from register. Reference Malfeasance Tribunal order three zero nine zero six. Subject—The Doctor.' Spandrell sat brooding for a moment, his heavy features set and grim. Unable to restrain his curiosity any longer, Engin wandered casually across to him. 'Can I be of any further help, Castellan Spandrell?'

'One moment, Co-ordinator.' Spandrell tapped out a code on his wrist-communicator. Seconds later the face of Hildred appeared on the tiny screen. 'Commander Hildred, Sector Seven.'

'Malfeasance, Hildred.'

'Castellan?'

'*Crime*. The occupant of your Type Forty is a convicted criminal known as "The Doctor". Approach with extreme caution.'

Hildred lowered his own viewer and turned to the waiting Guards at his side. 'You heard that? Set your stasers. Safety off.' The Guards adjusted the settings on their staser-guns. From now on, they would be shooting to kill. Hildred spoke into his communicator. 'I want armed reinforcements in Sector Seven. Immediately, please.'

The Doctor was writing a brief note on a sheet of parchment embossed with an elaborate seal. He finished, signed with a flourish, and glanced in the scanner. A Guard was approaching Hildred, carrying a flat leather case. As Hildred opened the lid, the Doctor glimpsed row upon row of keys set into the black velvet lining. He smiled ruefully. On any other planet in the Universe the TARDIS was invulnerable. But not on Gallifrey—the planet on which it had been made.

He flung open a nearby locker, and started rummaging through it in search of inspiration. Somewhere near the bottom, he found a dusty cardboard box, with Turkish lettering on the lid. 'Cash and Carry, Constantinople,' translated the Doctor. An idea was forming in his mind. 'After all,' he thought, 'it worked for old Sherlock ...'

The Doctor touched a control, and the lights slowly

dimmed. From the cardboard box he took a hookah, an elaborate Turkish water-pipe with a long flexible stem. He carried it over to the high-backed armchair that stood near the console.

After several unsuccessful attempts, Hildred found exactly the right key, and turned it in the TARDIS lock. The door swung open. Staser-pistol in hand, Hildred moved cautiously into the TARDIS control room, armed Guards behind him.

Peering through the gloom, Hildred saw a high-backed chair on the far side of the control room. Its back was angled towards him, but he could just make out a relaxed figure lounging in the chair. It had a broad-brimmed hat tipped over its eyes, an immensely long scarf dangled from its neck and it seemed to be puffing at a complicated, long-stemmed pipe. The air above the chair was blue with smoke.

Hildred stepped forward, staser-pistol raised. 'Don't move!' The figure didn't move, and as Hildred came closer he saw why. The shape in the chair was no more than a pile of cushions, the hat was propped up against the chair-back, and the long flexible pipe-stem was held by a knot in the scarf. Deceived by the simplest of illusions, Hildred had seen what he expected to see.

(The Doctor crouched motionless in the shadows behind the console. As Hildred and his Guards crowded round the chair, he rose silently and edged his way towards the door.)

There was a square of white pinned to one of the

16

cushions—a note. Hildred snatched it up. He was about to read it when he saw a flicker of movement on the TARDIS scanner. A tall figure was disappearing into the darkness of the Cloisters. 'There he goes!' shouted Hildred. 'After him!' Guards at his heels, Hildred dashed from the TARDIS.

The Doctor sprinted along the Cloisters trying desperately to recall boyhood memories of forbidden games, of hide-and-seek. Now, if he could get into the main tower by one of the service lifts ... He turned a corner, and there was the lift-door, right in front of him. He touched the call button and there was a faint hum of power. A moment later the lift doors slid open—to reveal a Guard, staser-gun at the ready. The first of Hildred's reinforcements had arrived.

The Guard raised his rifle. The Doctor stepped back, thinking this must be the shortest and most unsuccessful escape of his career.

A staser-gun crackled, and the Guard staggered sideways and toppled out of the lift. The Doctor turned, caught a fleeting glimpse of a cowled figure disappearing into the darkness. 'Stop!' he called ... but the figure was gone. As the Doctor turned to look at the body of the Guard, he heard shouts and the clatter of booted feet.

Hildred and his Guards were almost upon him— and he was standing over the dead body of one of their fellows ...

2

The Secret Enemy

The Doctor hesitated for no more than a moment. The death of the Guard made flight more urgent than ever. No one would believe in his innocence. He'd be lucky if he wasn't shot down on the spot.

Leaning forward, the Doctor stretched out a long arm, and pressed one of the control buttons inside the lift ...

Hildred and his men ran up just in time to see the lift doors close. After a brief examination of the Guard's body, Hildred straightened up, his face grim. 'He's got into the main tower. We'll have to search every floor.'

He raised his communicator. 'All Guards report to Main Tower, Sector Seven. Armed and dangerous intruder at large! You are authorised to shoot on sight!'

The Doctor, however, wasn't in the lift. He'd sent it speeding, empty, to the top floor of the tower. Now, hiding in the shadows around the corner, he slipped quietly away.

Co-ordinator Engin sat hunched over a read-out terminal studying the flickering of symbols across the screen. Spandrell looked on impatiently. Information in this category was automatically encoded, but Engin had worked so long with the computer that he could sight-read the symbols. Spandrell was in a hurry and he found it infuriating that all his information had to be filtered through the sometimes wandering mind of the ancient Co-ordinator.

Engin screwed up his eyes as he peered at the symbols. 'Now, let me see ... It appears that in view of certain extenuating circumstances, the Tribunal chose to impose a lenient sentence.'

'*What?*' asked Spandrell impatiently.

Literal as one of his own computers, Engin began again. 'In view of certain extenuating circumstances ...'

'No, no, Co-ordinator. I meant what *sentence*?'

Engin chuckled wheezily. 'I do beg your pardon. It appears the sentence was one of ... exile to Earth!'

'Earth?' Spandrell had never heard of the place.

'Sol 3—in Mutters Spiral. Interesting little planet, I understand. Been visited by several of our graduates ...'

'Is there any further information—anything *relevant*?'

A fresh line of symbols appeared on the screen. 'There is a rather interesting addendum, Castellan. It seems the sentence was subsequently remitted. The Doctor was given a complete pardon—at the intercession of the Celestial Intervention Agency.'

Spandrell looked up sharply. This gave the whole affair a new and worrying dimension. The whole basis of Time Lord philosophy was that there must be no interference in the affairs of the Universe. Yet from time to time such interference was thought urgently necessary. These operations were under the control of an ultra-secret Agency, composed of Time Lords of the highest rank, and they were always shrouded in mystery. 'Does it say why the Agency interceded?'

'I'm afraid not. All it says here is, "Refer to Omega file"—and that's restricted. High Council only.'

Spandrell had been on a remote province of Gallifrey at the time, but the effects of the terrible Omega crisis had been felt even there. The attack from some unknown all-powerful enemy, the crippling energy-drain that had almost destroyed the planet—then suddenly it was all over, and everyone was pretending it had never happened. Only the President and a few members of the High Council knew the full story. If the intruder had been mixed up in an affair of such magnitude, he was no ordinary criminal.*

Perhaps the Doctor's early life would provide some clue, thought Spandrell. 'Can you get me his biographical extract?'

'Certainly. It'll take a moment or two to withdraw it from the files.'

Engin went to a panel in the wall nearby, and began adjusting controls. As Spandrell waited impatiently, he saw Hildred moving hesitantly towards him. He could tell by the expression of the young Commander's face that the news wasn't good.

Hildred was a conscientious young officer and he felt it his duty to report his failure in person. He came to a halt before Spandrell and saluted. 'Castellan, I

* See 'Doctor Who—The Three Doctors'.

have to report that in the matter of the intruder in Sector Seven ...'

'Well? Where *is* he?'

Hildred gulped. 'He evaded us, Castellan. He shot one of my Guards.'

Spandrell closed his eyes briefly, as if in pain. 'I see. Such efficiency.'

'We have him trapped in the main Communications Tower, Castellan ...'

'Well done, Hildred!' said Spandrell bitingly. 'You receive adequate early warning that an antiquated capsule is about to arrive in your section—in the very heart of the Capitol. You are then informed that the occupant is a known criminal ... whereupon you allow him to escape and conceal himself in a building a mere fifty-three stories high. A clever stratagem, Hildred. I take it you're trying to confuse him?'

Hildred winced under the blast of sarcasm. 'My apologies, Castellan. The responsibility is mine. He won't escape capture again.'

Spandrell sighed. 'Let us hope not. In view of your record so far, you'd better not make rash promises.'

Hildred was holding out a square of parchment. 'I found this inside the capsule, Castellan.'

Spandrell took the note and read it aloud. '"To the Castellan of the Chancellery Guard: I have good reason to believe that the life of His Excellency the President is in danger. Do not ignore this warning— The Doctor."' He held the note up to the light. 'I see he's signed it over the Prydonian seal.'

There was a whoosh of compressed air and a muted chime. Engin opened a circular metal hatch in the wall and took out a silvery tube with a red cap. 'Indeed? Well, he has every right to do so. It appears that your intruder is—or was—a member of that noble Chapter.'

'How can you tell?'

Engin tapped the red cap. 'All biographies are colour coded according to Chapter.'

Spandrell took the cylinder and stared at it thoughtfully. 'Are they now? I had no idea ...'

Engin gave a wheezy chuckle. 'No? I suppose your duties usually involve you with more plebeian classes, eh, Castellan?'

Spandrell smiled ruefully. There was more than a little truth in the old Co-ordinator's jibe. The Time Lords were themselves a kind of aristocracy. Relatively few inhabitants of Gallifrey were of Time Lord rank. And this élite group was itself sub-divided into a number of societies or Chapters, Prydonians, Arcalians, Patrexes, and so forth. The members of each Chapter were bound together by a complex web of family and political alliances, and by one over-riding purpose—to compete with all the rival Chapters. And of all the different Chapters, the Prydonians were the most aristocratic, the most powerful, and the most ruthless.

The Castellan tapped the little silver tube against his palm. 'A Prydonian renegade, eh? We're in deep waters, Hildred. I think I'd better refer this to Chancellor Goth.'

The Doctor found it relatively easy to elude the departing Guards. Convinced he was already inside the Tower, they made no attempt to look for him in the Cloisters. He made his way quietly back to the TARDIS and slipped inside. As the door closed behind him, a black-cowled figure watched from the shadows. Its voice was a dry, rasping croak. 'As ingenious as ever, Doctor—and as predictable.' The cowled figure glided away, swallowed up by darkness.

Spandrell always felt clumsy and out of place in the Chancellor's office, surrounded by marble columns, silken hangings and fine mosaics. Behind an immense, ornately-carved desk, Chancellor Goth listened to Spandrell's account of the mysterious intruder.

Goth was tall, handsome, immensely impressive in his elaborate robes. There was no sign on his impassive face that he was worried, or even particularly interested by the story.

'This Doctor seems to be a Prydonian renegade,' Spandrell concluded. 'When a Prydonian forswears his birthright, there can be little else he fears to lose —isn't that so, sir?'

Goth nodded slowly. He was a Prydonian himself, and knew the truth of Spandrell's remark. 'So you think the danger is real?'

'He's already killed one of my Guards. I think he's ruthless and determined, sir. And if he's involved with the Agency ...'

'That's just it, Castellan. If he *is* in their service, why should he wish to harm the President?'

Spandrell shrugged. 'He could have been suborned by some outside force. If he's been false to his Prydonian vows his fidelity is already suspect.'

'But the note,' persisted Goth. 'Why warn us in advance?'

'To put us off balance—get us looking the wrong way for some reason. Prydonians are notoriously——' He broke off.

Goth gave one of his rare smiles. 'Devious, Castellan? Not so. We merely see a little further ahead than most. Now then, what is it that you want from me?'

'Your permission to withdraw fifty Guards from the Panopticon—to help search the Communications Tower.'

'It will mean a certain loss of pomp and ceremony...'

Spandrell sighed. An assassin on the loose, and the Chancellor was worrying about appearances. 'I'm afraid so, Chancellor. But I'll feel happier once this intruder is in custody.'

'Very well, Castellan. If you must...'

Spandrell bowed. 'Thank you, sir.' He began a hasty withdrawal, before the Chancellor could change his mind.

Goth detained him, a hand on his arm, 'I'd rather like to see this—TARDIS, you called it? Extraordinary to think an old Type Forty could still be operational.'

'It's in the Cloisters, sir. Sector Seven.'

To Spandrell's surprise, the Chancellor accompanied him towards the door. 'Then we'll have to hurry. I have an audience with the Cardinals in a few minutes.' Cardinals were the senior officials of the various rival Chapters. They played a vital part in the complex organisation of the Resignation Day Ceremonies. Spandrell bowed resignedly, and followed the Chancellor from the room.

The Doctor fiddled irritably with the tuner of his scanner. 'I've got to know more about what's going on ... Now, where's that local news circuit ... ah!'

The interior of the Panopticon Hall appeared on the little screen. This immense, circular chamber, used by the Time Lords for all major ceremonies, occupied the entire central dome of the Panopticon. Row upon row of viewing galleries ran round the walls. The marble floor was big enough to hold an army, the domed glass roof so high overhead that one lost all sensation of being indoors. On the far side of the hall, an enormous staircase led from the robing rooms down onto the central dais. Here the President would finally appear, to announce his resignation, and name his successor.

The Doctor saw that the camera was set up on one of the upper service galleries. From this height the figures on the floor of the Panopticon looked like animated chessmen, as the officials of the various Chapters, gorgeous in their multi-coloured robes, filed into position on the floor of the Chamber.

A solemn voice was commentating on the proceedings. 'Around me on the floor, and in the high galleries of the Panopticon, the Time Lords are already gathering in their ceremonial robes with the traditional colourful collars. The orange and scarlet of the Prydonians, the green of the Arcalians, the heliotrope of the Patrexes, and many others ... The one question that is on all their lips, the question of the day as his Supremacy leaves public life—who will he name as his successor?'

The camera zoomed in on a small plump figure standing by the main door of the Panopticon. The Doctor groaned. 'I might have known. It's Runcible! Runcible the fatuous ...'

Long, long ago, Runcible and the Doctor had been at school together. Even in those days Runcible had been utterly fascinated by rituals and traditions. No wonder he'd finished up in Public Record Video, the one position that would allow him to attend as many ceremonies as he liked.

With pompous reverence, Runcible continued his commentary. 'Approaching now is Cardinal Borusa, Leader of the Prydonian Chapter—the Chapter that has produced more Time Lord Presidents than all other Chapters together—and perhaps he will give us his answer to the vital question.'

A tall, hawk-faced old man, in the robes of a High Cardinal, was sweeping across the floor, flanked by a group of lesser officials. His face was seamed and wrinkled, and his hair snowy white, but his bearing was still upright and his eyes sparkled with intelligence. This was Cardinal Borusa, one of the most eminent figures in Time Lord public life. He had twice been offered the office of President, and had twice refused. The Presidential post had too many purely ceremonial functions. Borusa preferred to exercise real authority from behind the scenes.

The Doctor saw Runcible step forward. 'Cardinal Borusa, if you could spare a moment, sir——'

Borusa stopped and looked down at Runcible in mild astonishment. 'Yes?'

'Public Register Video, sir. If I could have a few words?'

Borusa peered keenly at him. 'Good gracious! Runcible, is it not?'

Runcible smiled, flattered at the recognition. 'That's right, sir.'

Borusa turned to the others. 'Runcible was one of my old pupils at the Prydonian Academy.'

'May I offer my congratulations on your recent elevation to High Cardinal, sir?'

'Thank you, Runcible. Good day to you.' Borusa moved on. As far as he was concerned, the interview was over.

Runcible scurried after him. 'Wait, sir—if I could just ask you a few questions——'

Irritated by this second interruption, the formidable old man snapped, 'Runcible, you had ample opportunity to ask me questions during your singularly mis-spent years at the Academy. You failed to avail yourself of the opportunity then, and it is too late now. Good day!'

Borusa strode off, followed by his entourage. For a moment Runcible was totally deflated, reduced to a delinquent schoolboy. Then he took a deep breath and smiled winningly into the unseen camera. 'I'm afraid Cardinal Borusa cannot, at this present point in time, commit himself to a reply. However, according to my own sources, Chancellor Goth, senior member of the Prydonian Chapter, and present number two in the High Council, is the widely fancied candidate.' Runcible paused and looked round. 'Approaching now are the Cardinals of the Patrexes Chapter ...'

Runcible droned on, but the Doctor wasn't listening. His eyes were fixed on the grand staircase. Down that staircase soon would come the President ...

The assassin pressed the trigger. The President crumpled and fell ...

Angrily the Doctor shook his head, and the vision faded. The ceremony hadn't started yet, the assassination hadn't happened. Somehow the Doctor had to get out of the TARDIS and stop his terrible vision from becoming reality.

3

Death of a Time Lord

In the Panopticon, Runcible was still droning on. 'Oh, shut up,' said the Doctor irritably and switched back to scan the Cloisters outside the TARDIS. All was still and silent, mist drifting eerily between the arches.

Three figures appeared out of the gathering darkness. Castellan Spandrell and Chancellor Goth walked side by side, Hildred following respectfully behind them.

As they approached, Goth was saying, 'I take it there is no way the intruder can enter the Panopticon from the Tower?'

Spandrell shook his head. 'Not without the help of an accomplice.'

As they came to a halt before the TARDIS, Goth said, 'You're suggesting there may also be a traitor within?'

'Perhaps the Doctor has gone inside the Tower to shake off the Guards, while someone else lifts the barriers that will admit him to the Panopticon.'

'What an inventive, suspicious mind you have, Spandrell. Though I suppose it's natural, in your position ...' Goth studied the TARDIS.

'So this is a Type Forty? Fascinating!'

'The shape is intended to be infinitely variable.

Chancellor. This one seems to have got stuck.'

'Yet it's still operational. Remarkable! What are you going to do with it?'

'I hadn't really thought. I've been more concerned with the occupant.'

'Well, I shouldn't leave it standing here—he might try to sneak back inside. Have it transducted to the Panopticon Museum. Most appropriate place, eh?' With a nod, Goth strode away.

Spandrell turned to Hildred. 'Get a transducer operator here right away.' Hildred used his wrist-communicator, and a few minutes later an overalled technician appeared, carrying a heavy box. From it he produced four black discs, magnetic terminals, which he attached to the TARDIS. He raised his communicator. 'Transduce to Capitol Museum—now.'

Somewhere inside the Communications Tower, another technician operated controls, the transducer beam locked on, and the TARDIS vanished slowly in sections—top left-hand corner, top right-hand corner, bottom left-hand corner—the final section, and it was gone.

Inside the Panopticon Museum, the TARDIS re-appeared, section by section, just as it had vanished. The door opened and the Doctor staggered out, hands to his head. 'What a way to travel,' he thought indignantly. Satisfied that, like the TARDIS, he'd arrived in one piece, the Doctor looked round. He was in a big gloomy room, filled with glass cases, holding all kinds of strange objects. The place was obviously a storeroom for items not currently on display. The Doctor rubbed his chin. At least he was inside the Panopticon. The next step was to get to the main hall without being captured. The Doctor looked at the strange collection of objects all round him. There were old carvings, bits of regalia, even an old grandfather clock. Just beside it was a dusty glass display case. It held a kind of rudimentary dummy, wearing elaborate golden ceremonial robes. The Doctor smiled ...

Deep beneath the Archive Tower two allies were conferring in a hidden chamber. One stood by the doorway, wrapped in a black cloak, the other sat, robed and cowled, in a high-backed stone chair. The room was in darkness, and any observer would have seen only two dark shapes, talking in low voices.

'So,' hissed the huddled shape in the chair. 'He is within the Capitol?'

'All his actions are exactly as you predicted, Master.'

'I know him,' croaked the cowled figure. 'I know him of old.'

'And are you sure he will succeed in reaching the Panopticon?'

'Of course. The Doctor is very resourceful. He knows he is entering a trap—but how can he resist such a bait.'

'The hope of preventing an assassination?'

'Exactly. Quixotic fool. He will die quickly.'

The Master leaned forwards, and the watcher by the door shrank back at the sight of the crawling horror of his ravaged features. The cracked, wizened skin, stretched tight over the skull, one eye almost closed, the other wide open and glaring madly. It was like the face of death itself, he thought.

'Remember,' insisted the Master, 'afterwards he must die *quickly*. See to it!'

The figure by the door bowed, and moved away.

Spandrell waited impatiently by the Cloister lift, as the door opened and Hildred emerged. 'Well?'

'We checked the entire tower, Castellan. All fifty-three floors. Nothing.'

Spandrell snorted. 'It's hardly surprising. I've been doing some checking myself. Take a look at this. Guard!'

At Spandrell's shout a Guard hurried forward, carrying a wide-barrelled, torch-like device. This was a track-tracer, a device which could follow the recent passage of living beings over inanimate material. It produced a high-pitched wailing sound which varied in volume with the strength of the track.

At a nod from Spandrell, the Guard demonstrated the Doctor's movements—up to the lift, and then away, over to the dark corner.

'He never even went into the lift,' whispered Hildred. 'He just doubled back.'

'That's right,' said Spandrell wearily. 'Back to the capsule. It's the only place for him to go. You'd better come with me, Hildred.' He turned to the Guard. 'You too. We'll need your tracker.'

Spandrell raised his communicator. 'Transduction section? I want to know *exactly* where you sent that capsule. Yes, the Type Forty from the Cloisters.'

Hildred and the Guard behind him, Spandrell led the way into the museum and up to the TARDIS. He nodded to the Guard, who began scanning with the tracker. The wailing sound led them away from the TARDIS and over to a glass case.

It was labelled 'Gold Usher,' and a placard inside explained the important part which this official took in many ceremonies. But instead of high-collared golden robes, the dummy in the case was wearing a loose roomy jacket. A long scarf dangled from its neck, and a floppy broad-rimmed hat perched on its round, featureless head.

Spandrell said grimly, 'Now we know how he plans to get into the Panopticon Hall.'

'But the Guards—everyone has to show a pass.'

'Do you think they'll stop Gold Usher?' snarled Spandrell. 'Would you, Hildred? Get over there and find him.'

'Right away, Castellan!' Beckoning to the Guard, Hildred set off at a run.

'And Hildred,' called Spandrell, 'try to be discreet!'

Hildred had already gone. Spandrell sighed and plunged his hands into the pockets of his tunic. He felt an unfamiliar shape and drew it out. It was a red-capped silver tube—the Doctor's biographical capsule. Perhaps somewhere in the intruder's past there was a clue to his present purpose. Trying to forget his aching feet, Spandrell set off for the Achives section.

In a velvet-curtained robing area, close to the main

hall of the Panopticon, two very old Time Lords were changing into ceremonial robes, and holding a vague conversation. 'You know,' said one, proudly, '*I* can remember the inauguration of Pandak the Third.' As he spoke, he was struggling out of his everyday robes. The ceremonial robes of a Prydonian Cardinal hung on a special stand nearby—that is, until a long gold-clad arm appeared from behind the curtains and lifted them quietly off.

The second Time Lord nodded vaguely, 'Pandak the Third, eh? Well, well . . .'

'Nine hundred years *he* lasted, you know. Now there was a President with some staying power.' The old Time Lord looked round at the empty stand. 'Where's my gown? I could have sworn it was here a moment ago.' He looked in total bafflement at the now empty stand. He became aware of a figure slipping through the curtains, and standing behind him. 'Here you are, sir.'

Grateful for the unexpected help, the old Time Lord slipped his arms into the offered robe, settling it onto his shoulders. His mind was still on the past. 'Thank you, my dear fellow, most awfully kind.' He settled the robe on his shoulders, as the tall figure slipped away. 'Nine hundred years,' he repeated. 'Bit different from these fellows today, chopping and changing every couple of centuries.' He noticed his fellow Time Lord staring at him. 'Anything the matter?'

'Well—you're *not* Gold Usher, are you?'

The Time Lord sighed. Clearly his old friend was getting a bit past it. 'Of course I'm not! I'm a Prydonian Cardinal, you know that.' He looked down at his robe and was astonished to find it gold, instead of the familiar orange and scarlet. 'I say,' he spluttered indignantly, 'that fellow's given me the wrong gown.'

'What fellow?'

The old Time Lord pulled back the heavy drapes. But the Doctor had gone.

The automatic Public Record Video camera was still functioning, perched on its ledge in the upper service gallery. But there was no sign of the technician who should have been looking after it.

On the wide shelf formed by the balcony edge, two black-gloved hands were expertly assembling a light staser-rifle. Stock, barrel, energy-cylinder and telescopic sight were all clipped efficiently into place.

When the rifle was complete, the black-cowled figure rested its elbows on the balcony edge beside the camera. Through the telescopic sights it began scanning the ever-growing crowd on the floor down below it. It amused the Master to think that with a gentle pressure on the trigger he could bring death to any one he chose.

Spandrell tapped the silver tube and looked at the old Co-ordinator. 'There must be *something* in his history, *some* clue. If I can convince Chancellor Goth that the threat is serious . . .'

'My dear Castellan, it would have to be very serious before they'd delay the Ceremony at this late date.

By now the President must be well on his way to the Panopticon. Still if you'll pass me the data-coil ...'

Spandrell took the red cap off the tube and shook out the double-spiral of fine silver wire upon which all the known details of the Doctor's lives were micro-encoded. He was about to pass it over when he paused, peering closely at it. 'This has been in a reader—very recently!'

'Surely not. If your intruder has just arrived ...'

Spandrell held up the coil. 'Look! No trace of mica dust.'

'There are millions upon millions of extracts in the data-files, Castellan. It's hardly feasible that some-one would chose to extract this particular one *before* the intruder arrived—and since then, it has been in your hands.'

'I live with the dirt of the past, Co-ordinator. And I can tell you, the dust of old crimes besmirches the fingers.'

Engin shook his head in puzzlement. 'Well if it has been withdrawn there'll certainly be a record. I can run a trace if you like.'

'I'd certainly like to know who had it. But the extract itself is more urgent. Let's see that first.'

'A pleasure, Castellan.' Engin slipped the silver coil into a reader, and the Doctor's lives began to flow across the screen.

The wandering telescopic sight froze on a tall figure in Prydonian robes, entering the Panopticon Hall by a side door.

There was a dry, rasping chuckle. 'There he is at last. The innocent to the slaughter!'

The Doctor looked round the crowded hall, and was appalled to see Hildred and a squad of Guards coming through the main door. With any luck they would still be looking for Gold Usher. But the Doctor felt conspicuous on his own, and he looked quickly round for someone to talk to.

A small plump figure stood rather disconsolately by the wall. Runcible had finished his preliminary transmission, and now had nothing to do until the ceremony proper began. The Doctor marched up to him and flung a friendly arm around his shoulders. 'Runcible my dear fellow! How nice to see you again.' With a gentle but remorseless pressure he swung Runcible round so they were facing away from the approaching Guards.

Runcible looked up at the Doctor in some annoyance. 'I'm sorry, I don't believe I recall ...'

The Doctor looked hurt. 'I know it's a long time since we were at the Academy together. And of course, I've changed a good deal. But surely you remember me? They used to call me the Doctor ...'

Runcible frowned. 'I still don't believe ... I say, weren't you expelled or something? No, not expelled, I remember you at graduation. But you were involved in some scandal, later on ...'

Cursing Runcible's too-accurate memory the Doctor said hurriedly, 'Oh that's all forgiven and forgotten now, old chap. Back in the fold!'

'Really?' said Runcible sceptically. 'And where have you been all these years?'

'Oh, here and there. Round and about, you know.'
As the Doctor spoke he was gazing over Runcible's
shoulder, following the progress of Hildred and his
Guards as they forced their way through the ever-
growing crowd.

Runcible sensed his distraction. 'Is something the
matter?'

'No, nothing, nothing. I get the odd twinge occa-
sionally.'

'Well, if you will lead such a rackety life,' said
Runcible disapprovingly. 'I suppose you've already
had several regenerations?'

'Yes, quite a few, I'm afraid ...'

Runcible felt he'd spent enough time on this odd
and probably rather shady figure from the distant past.
'Well,' he said insincerely, 'nice to have talked to
you. Must get on. I'm doing the Public Record Video-
cast, you know. We resume transmission soon.'

The Doctor saw that Hildred had paused and was
looking all around him. He laid a detaining hand
on Runcible's arm. 'I know—and I think you're doing
an absolutely *splendid* job.'

'Do you really think so?' Runcible couldn't help
feeling pleased. All too many Time Lords treated the
Public Record Video as a pointless nuisance.

'I do indeed,' said the Doctor earnestly. 'You've got
a natural gift, you know. Somehow you have a marvel-
lous way of making the whole thing come alive.'

There was a sudden fanfare, and Runcible
panicked. 'The President's arrived outside the Panopticon. He'll be coming down the main stair at any

moment.' He raised his wrist-communicator and jabbed at the controls.

The Doctor was staring into space. *The President jerked back and crumpled to the ground ...*

At this precise moment, the President was standing in the lift, surrounded by his retinue. The lift was carrying him to a corridor by the head of the great stairway, purely and simply so that he could make an impressive entrance, sweeping down the stairs and onto the central dais. An usher was handing him a smooth black rod, and settling the wide metallic links of the traditional Sash of Rassilon around his shoulders.

'You have everything you need, sir?' he asked discreetly. 'The list?'

'What? Oh, the Resignation Honours list.' The President touched a scroll inside his robes. 'Yes, here it is. One or two names in there will surprise them!'

The lift came smoothly to a halt, the doors opened and the President emerged into the antechamber at the head of the stairs. The usher nodded to a waiting aide. 'The President is ready. Let the ceremony begin!'

Runcible jabbed savagely at his communicator controls. 'Come on, *answer*, you stupid oick!'

The Doctor seemed to come to. 'What is it, Runcible? Having trouble?'

'No, my camera technician just isn't answering. I should be getting a signal from him—up there.'

Runcible pointed, and the Doctor looked up. High above the Panopticon Hall, on the topmost service gallery, he could see the squat shape of a video camera. The Doctor's eyes narrowed. And there was something else. *Projecting beside the camera was the barrel of a staser-rifle.*

'No!' shouted the Doctor. He set off across the floor of the Panopticon at a run, knocking Time Lords aside like skittles. Hands reached out to stop him, but he broke free of their hold. Dimly he remembered that this too had been part of his vision. 'They'll kill him!' Forcing his way through the crowd the Doctor made for the staircase that led to the service galleries.

Hildred's attention was attracted by the disturbance. He turned, just in time to see the Doctor disappearing. 'There he goes,' yelled Hildred. 'After him!' Followed by his Guards, Hildred too began forcing his way across the crowded hall.

The buzz of outraged comment from the assembled Time Lords was brought to a halt by another fanfare. Runcible remembered his duty. Hoping desperately that the video camera was still working, he began speaking softly into his communicator.

'There seems to have been some kind of disturbance here in the Panopticon Hall—no doubt we shall hear the full story later. Now the ceremony is about to begin. The members of the High Council, led by Chancellor Goth, are already assembled on the dais to greet his Supremacy the President ...'

Heart pounding, legs aching, the Doctor ran up and

up and up, ascending the service stairs at astonishing speed. He reached the top at last, and sprinted along the upper service gallery towards the video camera. Gasping for breath, he reached it at last ... and stopped in astonishment. The video camera hummed quietly on the edge of the balcony, the staser-rifle resting beside it. But there was no one in sight. Perhaps he'd already frightened the assassin away ...

The Doctor went forward and looked over the balcony. Below him was the main dais, and there was the President, making his stately way through the ranks of the High Council. The Doctor had an excellent view, though the balcony was so high above the dais that he could see little more of the President and High Council than the tops of their heads.

The members of the High Council were crowding round the President to greet him ... The Doctor could hear pounding feet as Hildred and his Guards ran along the gallery. The Doctor smiled, making no attempt to get away. He was still in a certain amount of trouble. But somehow he'd talk his way out of it. After all, what could they charge him with? Parking the TARDIS in a restricted zone? The main thing, he'd arrived in time. The President was safe.

Suddenly the Doctor tensed. Staring intently below him, he snatched up the staser-rifle, threw it to his shoulder, and fired. A staser-blast echoed through the Panopticon. The President jerked, staggered backwards. His lifeless body crumpled to the floor.

4

Trapped

The Doctor stood staring numbly down onto the floor of the Panopticon. It was a scene of utter chaos. Time Lords milled about in horrified panic, and on the dais, the members of the High Council crowded round the fallen President, hiding the body from view.

When Hildred's Guards burst into the service gallery, the Doctor was still standing there, the rifle in his hands. The leading Guard raised his staser-gun to fire. 'No!' shouted Hildred. 'Take him alive!'

The Doctor turned to run but now it was too late. The Guards hurled themselves upon him and there was a confused struggle. The butt of a staser-pistol took the Doctor behind the ear, and he fell at Hildred's feet.

On the dais, Goth was cradling the President's body in his arms. Runcible forced his way to the edge of the group. 'Did you see what happened, sir?'

The Chancellor shook his head dazedly. 'Not really. There was a shot, and the President fell. I was right beside him.'

Runcible turned to Cardinal Borusa. 'Is the President dead, sir?'

Even Borusa seemed stunned. 'I fear so. We live in terrible times.'

Runcible saw Spandrell shouldering his way through the crowd. 'Castellan Spandrell, can you tell us what's happening?'

Spandrell ignored him. 'Will you all keep back please? Make way!' Behind Spandrell came Hildred and his Guards, two of them half-dragging, half-carrying the semi-conscious figure of the Doctor. 'Is that him, Castellan?' asked Runcible excitedly. 'Is that the man?'

The Doctor was dragged up to the little group of High Councillors. Borusa looked at him incredulously. 'Is this the assassin? A Prydonian?'

Hildred said triumphantly, 'There's no possible doubt, sir. We found him in the camera-gallery. He was holding this.' He showed them the staser-rifle. There was an angry murmur from the crowd, and they began crowding around the Doctor. Spandrell turned to Hildred. 'Get him out of here, you fool. Put him in the detention sector.'

Suddenly the Doctor opened his eyes and gazed muzzily at Spandrell. 'Is the roof still there? I could have sworn it fell in on me!'

'Take him away,' ordered Hildred.

As the Guards dragged him out, the Doctor started to struggle. 'Wait! I can help you. I saw the whole thing ...' Still struggling and protesting, the Doctor was hauled away.

By now horrified Panopticon attendants were removing the President's body. Goth rose from beside the stretcher and beckoned to Spandrell. The

Chancellor's handsome face was cold and bleak. 'Castellan, the President is dead. The trial of the assassin will be held immediately.'

'I need more time, Chancellor.'

'Time for what?'

'There are unanswered questions. About the assassin, about his motives.'

'Such questions will be answered at the trial.'

Cardinal Borusa came across to join them. 'I agree with the Castellan, Chancellor. Too much haste is against all our traditions of justice.'

'This is no ordinary crime. This is a constitutional crisis. The President died before he could name his successor. In these circumstances, we are legally bound to hold an election within forty-eight hours.'

Borusa's legalistic mind refused to accept Goth's reasoning. 'The trial of the assassin, and the choice of the new President, are two separate issues,' he began ponderously.

Fiercely Goth interrupted him. 'Not so, Cardinal. This is a political matter. At the moment, the Time Lords are leaderless and in disarray. The assassin must be tried and executed *before* the election—to prove to Gallifrey that the High Council are still in control.'

Stripped of his borrowed Prydonian robes, the Doctor was in his shirt-sleeves, clamped to the walls of a metal cell, a fierce blue light playing into his eyes. The light came from a small torch-like device in the hands of Commander Hildred, and it seemed to burn into the

Doctor's brain. Sweat broke out on his face, and he twisted in pain. 'You will confess,' said Hildred remorselessly.

'All right,' gasped the Doctor. 'I confess!'

The light was shut off. 'Very sensible, Doctor.'

The Doctor smiled with dry lips. 'I confess you're a bigger idiot than I thought you were.'

Immediately the blue light was boring into his brain again. 'There are fifteen intensity settings on this device, Doctor,' snarled Hildred. 'At the moment you are only experiencing level nine. You would do better to talk.'

'I've ... nothing ... to say,' gasped the Doctor.

The light-beam stabbed at him again, more fiercely this time. Through a haze of pain he heard Hildred's voice. 'I'm sure you'll think of something soon.'

Spandrell came into the cell, and looked enquiringly at Hildred, who said eagerly, 'Just give me a little more time with him, Castellan.'

Spandrell said, 'Turn that thing off—and get out.' Hildred stamped out of the cell, slamming the door behind him. Spandrell looked after him with disgust. It was bad enough that they were sometimes forced to use such methods. To enjoy the process was unforgivable.

He crossed to the Doctor's slumped figure and lifted an eyelid. 'Are you all right?' Slowly the Doctor's eye focused and he said weakly, 'Tweedledee?'

Spandrell wondered if the interrogation had affected the Doctor's brain. 'I'm sorry?' He released the wall clamps and the Doctor sank weakly onto a metal bench. 'I must apologise for my subordinate,' said

Spandrell calmly. 'He lets his enthusiasm run away with him.'

'Tweedledum and Tweedledee,' muttered the Doctor. 'The hot and cold technique. You're not very original.'

'We're simply seekers after truth, Doctor. And we don't have very much time. Chancellor Goth has ordered your immediate trial.'

The Doctor rubbed his aching head. Despite the rough handling, he could feel his strength coming back. His mind was starting to work again. He looked at Spandrell. 'I'd like to help you, if I can. I suppose you'd like a signed confession?'

'That would be a help. I have a tidy mind, Doctor. Even when a conviction is certain, I hate to go into court without knowing all the facts. Motive, for instance.'

'Now there's a sensible question. Why should anyone want to murder a *retiring* President?'

'Some personal grudge?'

The Doctor smiled. 'I never met him.'

'I know Doctor. I scanned your biographical data.'

'And yet you still think I did it?'

'I think you're going to be executed for it,' said Spandrell calmly. 'They're preparing the vaporisation chamber at this very moment. You have about three more hours to live.'

The Doctor sat up. 'That's monstrous. Vaporisation without representation is against the constitution.'

'Well, frankly Doctor, you're a political embarrassment.'

The Doctor found that the prospect of execution

concentrated his mind wonderfully. 'You realise I've been framed, Castellan?'

'Framed?'

'Yes, *framed*. It's an Earth expression. It means someone has gone to a lot of trouble to get me into this mess.'

'All right, Doctor. Just how did someone "frame" you into being up in that gallery with a freshly fired staser-rifle in your hands?'

The Doctor told of the sequence of events that had led him to the gallery. 'I looked down on to the dais— *and saw one of the High Council take a staser-pistol from under his robes and aim at the President.* Don't ask me which one—I couldn't see their faces. *I shot at the assassin.* I missed—and he didn't.'

Spandrell looked thoughtfully at the Doctor. There was something strangely convincing about this renegade. 'Tell me, why *did* you come back to Gallifrey— if it wasn't to assassinate the President?'

'To save his life. If you remember I left a note— which, presumably you did nothing about?'

'I did all I could. So, you knew the President was going to be assassinated?'

'In a way, yes. I—experienced it.'

'Go on.'

The Doctor sighed. 'This is the bit you're not going to believe ...'

Co-ordinator Engin stared fascinatedly into the little screen of Spandrell's video-communicator. It was switched to playback, and on the tiny screen the Doctor was saying, 'This is the bit you're not going to believe. People talk of a premonition of tragedy, but I saw it happening. I saw the President die, as vividly, as clearly as I see this room now.'

Then Spandrell's own voice. 'And where were you when this happened?'

'In the TARDIS, travelling in Vortex. It was just after I'd heard the summons to the Panopticon.'

Spandrell switched off the communicator. 'Well, what do you think?'

The old Time Lord shook his head. 'True precognitive vision is impossible.'

'He knows that, and he knows we know it. Yet he maintains it happened—— And whatever he is, the Doctor isn't a fool.'

'So you believe this story of his?'

Almost reluctantly Spandrell said, 'I'm beginning to.'

'Nobody else will!'

'I think he's been framed.'

'Framed?'

'It's an Earth expression, Co-ordinator. You were going to run a check for me—on who'd withdrawn the Doctor's data coil recently.'

'Nobody had. I'm afraid you were wrong there Castellan.'

'I very much doubt it,' said Spandrell obstinately.

'The machine is virtually infallible. Data extraction is impossible without an operating key. The code of the particular key is recorded against the archive number of the data extract. My key is the only one recorded against the Doctor's number—when I withdrew the data at your request.'

'How many of these operating keys are there?'

'They are issued only to the High Council. No one else is allowed access to Time Lord data extracts ... except of course for yourself, Castellan, in the line of duty.'

'Suppose the record has been erased?'

Engin was shocked. 'Clearly, you have no idea of the complexity of exitonic circuitry.'

'No, I haven't. But suppose somebody else has—— Is it *possible*?'

'Theoretically yes. But it would require an unprincipled mathematical genius with an unparalleled knowledge of applied exitonics.'

Spandrell smiled wryly. 'Well, that narrows the field, Co-ordinator. There can't be many of those on the High Council.'

In the council hall of the Chancellery, the Cardinals were assembling for the Doctor's trial. Chancellor Goth sat at the head of the long table, Cardinal Borusa at his side. While the other Cardinals were taking their places, Goth and Borusa argued in low voices. 'I still feel we should allow time for reflection, Chancellor, time for passions to cool,' said Borusa stubbornly.

Goth's voice was unyielding. 'A wise and beloved President has been shot down in his last hours of office. No amount of reflection is going to alter that.'

'Nevertheless, in the present emotional climate,

there is danger that a violent action will cause an equally violent reaction.'

'I am aware of your concern for justice, Cardinal,' said Goth patiently. 'And of course I share it. But there are other considerations.' He paused, choosing his words. 'There is some possibility that, after the election, I shall have the honour of being President of the Council.'

'You're being over-modest, Chancellor,' said Borusa drily. 'Everyone knows the President would have named you as his successor. Everyone will feel that in electing you they are simply carrying out his wishes.'

Goth waved the compliment aside. 'Who can be sure what was in the President's mind? But that apart, it is our inviolable custom for an incoming President to pardon all political prisoners. Is the new President to pardon the murderer of his predecessor—or break with an age-old custom? Either course would be difficult. We can only avoid the dilemma by seeing that this sordid affair is concluded before the new President takes office.'

Borusa was unimpressed. '*All* Presidents must face difficult decisions, Chancellor. It is by their decisions that they are judged.'

Goth's face darkened, and he seemed about to make an angry reply. But at this moment the Doctor was brought in, and the Court Usher sounded the call for the trial to begin.

As the Doctor listened to the proceedings, he reflected that his trial wasn't likely to be a long one. With crisp efficiency, Spandrell told of the early warning that had alerted them to the Doctor's unauthorised arrival. Hildred told of his entry into the TARDIS, and of the unsuccessful search that had followed. He told of the hunt through the hall of the Panopticon, of discovering the Doctor in the service gallery, staser-rifle in hand, seconds after the President's death.

With the main story established, there followed various corroborating witnesses. Runcible told of meeting the Doctor in the Panopticon. 'I thought he seemed nervous, apprehensive. He was looking round all the time we were talking. Just before the President appeared, he started to run across the floor ...'

An old and indignant Time Lord told of the Doctor's mad dash to the staircase. 'He pushed past me in a loutish and unmannerly way. I caught his arm to remonstrate with him but he pulled away shouting, "Let me go. They'll kill him." '

Goth leaned forward. 'Forgive me sir, but are you perhaps getting a little hard of hearing?'

'At my age one must expect these things. I'm nearing the end of my twelfth regeneration, you know. As a matter of fact, I've been having trouble with my hip recently—and my back ...'

Goth cut across the list of symptoms. 'So the prisoner *might* have been saying, "Let me go, I'll kill him"?'

'Well, it's possible ... he *might* have said that ...'

For the first and only time in the trial the Doctor exercised his right to question witnesses. 'I believe you said I shouted, sir?'

'That's right.'

'And you can hear a *loud* voice clearly enough?'

'Yes, of course I can.'

'Thank you, sir,' said the Doctor and sat down again. For the remainder of the testimony he sat quietly, doodling on the pad in front of him.

When all the evidence had been given, Chancellor Goth conferred for a moment with his fellow members of the High Council. Then he looked sternly at the Doctor. 'Have you anything to say before our verdict is reached?'

Spandrell watched the Doctor get up. He wondered how the High Council would react, when the Doctor made his astonishing charge that the real assassin was one of their number. However, like everyone else in the Court, Spandrell was quite unprepared for what happened next.

The Doctor paused, looked round the room then spoke in a loud clear voice. 'I have only one thing to say. I wish to offer myself as a candidate for the Presidency of the High Council.'

5

The Horror in the Gallery

There was a moment of shocked silence—then pande-
monium. Goth's angry voice cut through the babble.
'*What* was that?'

'I offer myself as a candidate for the Presidency,'
repeated the Doctor. 'And I invoke Article Seventeen
of the Constitution ... the guarantee of liberty. No
candidate for office shall be in any way barred or
restrained from presenting his claim.'

'The guarantee of liberty does not extend to the
protection of assassins—you have no right to claim it.'

Borusa leaned forward, with an expression of
malicious enjoyment. 'Forgive me, Chancellor, but as
an expert in jurisprudence, I must disagree. The
accused has not yet been found guilty. Until he is, the
protection of Article Seventeen still applies.'

'He is using his cunning to abuse a legal tech-
nicality.'

The Doctor said cheerfully, 'Nonsense. I'm claiming a legal right.'

Borusa agreed. 'This trial must now stand adjourned
until after the election.'

There were many more angry protests from Chancellor Goth, but Borusa was immovable. The law was
the law. Finally Goth rose to his feet. 'Very well. It

appears that the prisoner must be set free until the election is over.' He looked menacingly at the Doctor. 'Do not think you will escape justice. Immediately after the election, you will be re-arrested, tried and executed. Castellan!'

Spandrell rose from his corner and came forward. Like Borusa he was sardonically amused by the turn of events—though, unlike Borusa, he didn't dare to show it. His face impassive, he said, 'Yes, Chancellor?'

'See the accused has no opportunity to leave the Capitol.'

Goth stormed out of the Courtroom, and the other Cardinals began filing after him. Spandrell went over to the Doctor, who was quietly doodling on his pad. 'Well, Doctor, you have forty-eight hours!'

The Doctor smiled wryly. 'It's a lot better than three, isn't it?'

'What are you going to do with the time?'

'Prove my innocence. Find the real assassin. If I can convince you I didn't do it—will you help me?'

Spandrell looked down at him. 'You know, I can't help admiring your audacity. Very well, Doctor— convince me!'

The Councillor descended the stone steps to the secret chamber where the cowled figure sat immobile in the high-backed chair. It might not have moved at all since the last time they met. 'Well?' croaked the rasping voice.

'The trial was adjourned, Master. He pleaded Article Seventeen, the clause of protection.'

He heard the sound of the Master's painful breathing ... 'He remains as ingenious as ever.'

'He will not escape for long.'

'Escape is not in his mind,' whispered the Master. 'Now he is hunting *you*!'

There was panic in the Time Lord's voice. 'It was a mistake to bring him here. We could have used anyone...'

'No. We could *not* have used anyone. You do not understand hatred, as I understand it. Only hate keeps me alive. Why else should I endure *this*?' The Master stretched out a hand that might have belonged to a mummified corpse, withered skin stretched tight across the bones. 'I *must* see the Doctor die in shame and dishonour, before I destroy the Time Lords. Nothing else matters. *Nothing* ...' The agonised whisper of hate drifted through the shadows of the underground room.

The Castellan and his staff occupied a set of old-fashioned chambers in an obscure corner of the Capitol, as plain and functional as Spandrell himself. The Doctor stood before a battered wooden table. On it rested the staser-rifle he had been holding when he was captured.

The Doctor picked up the rifle and Spandrell stepped back cautiously. 'I hope you're not planning anything ambitious, Doctor.' He nodded towards the door where Hildred stood with a knot of Guards.

'Wouldn't dream of it, old chap. I just wanted to

be sure it was the same rifle. Are you a good shot, Castellan?'

'It's part of my job.'

The Doctor nodded thoughtfully. 'Yes ... I'm a pretty good shot myself as it happens.' He pointed towards an old-fashioned light-globe set into the far wall of the long room. 'You see that light?'

'What about it?'

'Try to hit it.' He tossed the rifle to Spandrell, who caught it automatically. 'Go on—just try!'

Spandrell gave him a baffled look then raised the staser-rifle to his shoulder. 'People get run in for this sort of vandalism,' he muttered.

He peered through the telescopic sight and centered the glowing white dot on the light-globe. At this range the shot was ludicrously easy. Spandrell squeezed the trigger. The bark of the staser-blast *should* have been followed by the sound of shattering crystal. But it wasn't. He saw to his astonishment that the light-globe was still there on the wall. He moved closer. The scorch-mark of the staser-blast wasn't even on the wall. It was on the ceiling just above.

'The sights have been fixed,' said the Doctor simply. 'I couldn't have hit the President with that rifle if I tried. More important, I didn't hit the real assassin when I did fire. That's *why* the sights were fixed.'

There was now only one question in Spandrell's mind. '*Which* member of the High Council shot the President?'

'I told you—I was almost directly above. Those high collars hid their faces.'

'Why didn't you tell your story in court?'

'With the real assassin as one of my judges?'

Spandrell nodded, sinking wearily into a chair. 'So we're after one of the High Council? It's a good story, Doctor. But it's still only a story. Where's your evidence? The rifle isn't enough by itself.'

The Doctor was striding about the room. In his mind he was seeing the scene in the service gallery. The staser-rifle resting on the ledge, the deserted video camera humming quietly away ... 'I'll tell you where the evidence is,' he shouted. 'In the Public Register camera. I was standing right beside it. Blow up the image and we'll be able to identify the assassin ...'

Spandrell jumped up. 'Doctor, you may end up as President yet. Hildred, come over here. I want you to escort the Doctor to the Panopticon.'

'Now sir? It's late, it'll be closed up.'

'I'm aware of that. I'm going to get the Chancellor's authority to open it. I'll want Commentator Runcible as well. Get everyone over there and wait for me.'

Despite the late hour, Goth was still hard at work when Spandrell arrived at the Chancellery. He received the Castellan at once, and listened in astonishment to his request. 'You want the Panopticon opened —at this hour? That's rather unusual. For what reason?'

'Further investigation, sir,' said Spandrell woodenly. He had no intention of repeating the Doctor's wild story until there was solid evidence.

'I see. Well of course, Castellan, if you think there is any more to be discovered ... I'll give the necessary orders.'

'Thank you, sir.'

'You're keeping a close watch on this Doctor?'

'Someone with him all the time, sir.'

Goth was shuffling papers in evident irritation. 'You realise, Castellan that the Doctor and myself are the *only* candidates in this election?'

'Is that so, sir?'

'*I* am to compete with a renegade and a murderer! It exposes the highest office in the land to ridicule. My first action as President will be to order Cardinal Borusa to amend Article Seventeen. I'll see this sort of thing never happens again ...'

When Spandrell arrived at the Panopticon the Doctor, Runcible and Hildred were all waiting for him. A scandalised Panopticon attendant appeared to open the doors. Since the huge building was now in semi-darkness, Spandrell bullied the attendant into producing a supply of hand-lanterns. Armed with these they entered the cavernous darkness of the enormous hall, their footsteps echoing on the marble floor. They made their way on to the dais and stood grouped around the spot where the President had fallen. There was something curiously pathetic about the sprawled outline that marked the place of his death.

Runcible was protesting about being dragged out in the middle of the night. Spandrell told him why he was wanted.

'Well, it's not really my field,' said Runcible dubiously. 'My technician would normally handle that sort of thing.'

'Your technician has disappeared, Runcible,' said

Spandrell patiently. 'I take it you do have *some* technical knowledge? All I want to see is the sequence leading up to the actual assassination.'

'Yes ... well, I expect that will be stored in the last band of the drum.'

'Splendid,' said Spandrell sardonically. 'Then perhaps you will be kind enough to go and fetch it?'

'Er ... yes. Right, Castellan. Now?'

'If you please, Commentator Runcible.'

Runcible's light bobbed away as he set off for the stairs.

High above in the service gallery, a dark figure watched his approach.

The Doctor was studying the chalk outline. 'So, if the President was standing about here ... and the assassin about here ... and I fired from up there ... the bolt would have passed over his head, and to the left ...'

'Then let's look for the blaster mark,' said Spandrell practically. He shone his lantern. 'Somewhere across here, I should say ...'

'Castellan!' called Hildred.

'What is it?'

'I thought I heard movement up in the service gallery.'

'That's only natural, Commander. After all I've just sent Runcible up there. Now come and help search for this blaster-mark.'

Hildred obeyed, but he was still puzzled. If it *had* been Runcible—why hadn't he seen his lantern?

Runcible was glad when he finally reached the upper gallery. It had been an eerie journey, alone through the darkness. All the way along the service gallery he'd been thinking he heard—*sounds*.

He looked over the balcony and saw the lights of the others bobbing about down below. With a sigh, Runcible turned to the video camera. As far as he could see, no one had interfered with it. Clumsily he began unscrewing the drum that housed the recorder-bands.

It was Hildred who found the blaster mark. 'Here Castellan!' He shone his lantern at the point where the rear wall of the dais joined the floor.

They came across to join him, and the Doctor peered at the modest-sized scorch-mark. 'Is that it?'

'Stasers don't do a lot of damage—except to body tissue,' said Spandrell. 'Looking at the President's body, you couldn't say exactly where he was hit—too much damage.'

The Doctor shuddered at this rather gruesome piece of professional expertise. Still, at least they'd found the mark. One more piece of evidence to support his story.

Runcible finally unscrewed the heavy drum-lid and peered inside. His face twisted, and he screamed ...

Far below the Doctor and the others heard the scream.

The note of pure terror in the voice sent them running for the staircase.

Runcible lay huddled at the foot of the camera. He had fainted from sheer fright. Beside him, a black-cowled figure was rapidly sorting through the cassettes inside the drum.

There came a sound of running feet, and Spandrell's voice echoed down the service gallery. 'Runcible, where are you? Are you all right?' With a hiss of anger, the figure slipped away into the darkness.

A few minutes later, Spandrell appeared, the Doctor and Hildred close behind. He knelt beside Runcible's body, and the little commentator stirred, and gave a feeble moan.

'He's alive anyway,' said the Doctor. 'What happened, Runcible?'

'Horrible,' moaned Runcible. 'It's *horrible* ...'

'What happened?' demanded Spandrell.

Runcible struggled to sit up. 'My technician. He's in there—in the drum ...'

In one long stride the Doctor crossed to the camera and peered inside the drum. Spandrell looked over his shoulder.

Stuffed inside the drum was a tiny, twisted corpse.

6

Into the Matrix

Spandrell looked at the Doctor in baffled horror. 'What's happened to him?'

'Matter condensation,' said the Doctor briefly. 'It's a particularly revolting death.'

'No wonder we couldn't find him,' said Spandrell, and turned away in distaste. 'I've never seen anything like it.'

'I have, I'm afraid,' said the Doctor softly.

'You have? Where?'

'It's an unpleasant technique the Master acquired, somewhere on his travels. You might say it's a kind of trademark.'

'And who is the Master?'

'Who is the Master?' The Doctor swung round to face him. 'My sworn enemy, Castellan Spandrell. A fiend who glories in chaos and destruction. If he's back on Gallifrey ...'

'Back?' Spandrell pounced on the word. 'You mean he's a Time Lord?'

'He was—a long while ago. You know, a lot of things are suddenly becoming clearer.'

Spandrell gave him a long-suffering look. 'Not to me, they're not.'

'If the Master *is* here, this must be his final

challenge.' He gestured towards the technician's body. 'And *that* is just a sort of greetings card. A little joke.'

Spandrell wondered what kind of twisted mind could find humour in a shrunken corpse. 'Take that thing away, Hildred,' he ordered. 'First take the video cassettes out and give them to Commentator Runcible. Runcible, you find the one we need.'

Runcible took the cassettes from Hildred and Hildred screwed the lid back on the drum, and lifted it from the camera.

Runcible fumbled through the cassettes with shaking hands, while Spandrell watched him sourly. 'Well, have you found what we want?'

'This is the one, Castellan. You can tell by the numbers.'

'*I* can tell when I see it, and not before. Take it down to Records, I'll look at it there.'

'Right, Castellan.' Runcible took the cassette, climbed unsteadily to his feet and set off down the gallery.

Spandrell turned to the Doctor, 'I shall want to know everything you can tell me about this Master. And I warn you now, if there's some kind of private feud between you—don't try to settle it on Gallifrey.'

The Doctor was unimpressed by the threat in Spandrell's voice.

'It can't be avoided, Castellan,' he said sombrely. 'Like it or not, Gallifrey is involved. And it may never be the same again. Let me tell you a little about the Master ...'

As they walked along the darkened service gallery

63

and down the stairs, the Doctor gave Spandrell a brief summary of the Master's evil career.

'Mind you,' he concluded, 'that isn't the whole story by any means. I lost sight of the Master on Earth some time ago. There's no telling what he's been up to since then.'

Spandrell grunted. 'If he is, or was, a Time Lord, there'll be some kind of data extract in the files ...'

'Perhaps,' said the Doctor thoughtfully.

'What do you mean, perhaps?' grumbled Spandrell. 'A full biography is kept on every ...' He broke off as a small, plump figure came towards them. 'Runcible? What's the matter?'

Runcible stumbled slowly forward, his empty hands held out, as if in apology. 'The cassette ... Somebody ... some——' He fell forward onto his face. From between his shoulder-blades projected the handle of a knife.

'Four cold-blooded killings in one day!' said Spandrell explosively. Too restless to sit down, he strode up and down between the data banks of the Record Section.

Sprawled in Engin's favourite chair, the Doctor seemed totally relaxed. 'Fleabites, Spandrell,' he said with gloomy relish. 'We've hardly started yet. Things will get worse before they get better.'

'Here—in the Capitol?' Spandrell was appalled.

'Well, perhaps it will shake a few Time Lords out of their lethargy. They live for centuries and they have as much sense of adventure as dormice!'

Looking very like an old white dormouse himself,

Co-ordinator Engin came scurrying between his data banks. 'I'm afraid there's nothing, Castellan. No record of any Time Lord who ever adopted the title of "Master".'

'Told you,' said the Doctor unrepentantly. 'If there was a data extract on the Master, destroying it would be his first move.'

'Indeed? Yet the Co-ordinator here assures me that Time Lords Data extracts cannot be withdrawn, without the fact being recorded. I thought someone had scanned *your* extract, Doctor, but apparently that's impossible.'

'Rubbish,' said the Doctor vigorously. 'Simple for anyone with a little criminal know-how. Even I could do it.'

Engin cackled disbelievingly. 'You would need more than *criminal* know-how, Doctor. Advanced exitonic circuitry of this kind ...'

The Doctor jumped to his feet. 'Child's play to the Master. You think this is a sophisticated system?' The Doctor waved a dismissive hand at the rows of data banks. 'There are planets out there where this sort of thing would be considered prehistoric.'

The Doctor's attack on his beloved Records Section made old Engin splutter with rage. 'Of all the arrogant, unmitigated rubbish ...'

Hurriedly Spandrell asked the Doctor, 'What's the Master like on mathematics?'

The Doctor was prowling restlessly about the Record Section as if searching for some clue. 'Absolutely brilliant. Almost up to my standard.' He paused before a corner area where complex data banks surrounded a low couch. The couch itself seemed to be wired into a nearby console. 'What's all this?' he demanded.

Engin hobbled over. 'One of our prehistoric pieces of equipment,' he said acidly. 'It's the A.P.C. Section.'

'A.P.C.?'

'Amplified Panotropic Computations.'

The Doctor nodded. 'In other words—brain cells!'

Engin fixed him with a reproving eye. 'Trillions of electro-chemical cells in a continuous matrix, a master-pattern. At the moment of death an electrical scan is made of the brain pattern and these millions of impulses are immediately transferred ...'

'Yes, yes, the theory's simple enough,' said the Doctor impatiently. 'What's the function?'

'The Matrix is a huge communal brain. It monitors the life of the Capitol, and makes provision for the future. We use its accumulated wisdom and experience to predict future events and to plan how to deal with them.'

'What about the assassination of the President?'

'For some reason that was not foreseen,' said the old Co-ordinator sadly.

The Doctor was suddenly jubilant. 'Oh yes it was, my dear old Engin. It was foreseen by *me*! Oh that's very clever. He's really surpassed himself this time!'

Spandrell was beginning to lose patience. 'What *are* you talking about, Doctor?'

'Don't you see? Time Lords are telepathic, and this thing here is a very complex brain. The Master intercepted its forecast of the assassination and beamed it into my mind.'

66

Spandrell was bemused. 'Is that even possible?'

'Yes,' said the Doctor, positively. 'Yes, the Master could do it. Spandrell, you say you thought my data extract had been scanned?'

'Yes. There was no mica-dust.'

'He'd need my biography print to beam a message accurately over such a distance ... it all hangs together, Spandrell.'

'Maybe. Why would the Master want you to know his plan?'

'I told you. He's got a lot of old scores to settle.'

Engin was still unconvinced. 'Doctor, I simply do not believe that anyone could do what you are suggesting. How can one intercept thought-patterns within the Matrix itself?'

'By going in there—joining it?'

'A living mind?' asked Spandrell incredulously.

'Why not? In a sense that's all a living mind is— electro-chemical impulses.' The Doctor paused. 'And if I went in there myself I could track him down and destroy him ...'

Engin shook his head. 'I couldn't allow it. The psychosomatic feedback might very well kill you. The thing's never been done before ... far too dangerous.'

'It's better than being vaporised, Co-ordinator. That's what's waiting for me if I don't go in.'

Engin looked worriedly at Spandrell. The Castellan nodded. 'Let him try it. He's got very little to lose.'

Engin remained dubious, but at last they managed to persuade him. 'Very well,' he sighed. 'If you'll lie down on the couch, Doctor.'

The Doctor stretched out, and Engin began applying a variety of electrodes to his head and body. 'Is this what happens to the near-deceased?' asked the Doctor cheerfully.

Engin gave a rather embarrassed cough. 'Well yes —though they are normally unconscious. This will be a considerable shock to your system, Doctor. There may be some pain ...'

The Doctor braced himself. 'I'm ready when you are.'

Engin still hesitated. 'You're *sure* you want to do this?'

The Doctor didn't want to do it in the least, but he could see no alternative. 'Oh get on with it!'

Engin threw a switch, and the Doctor's body arched as though electrocuted. For a moment his entire body was bent like a bow. Then it slumped back onto the couch, the breathing so shallow that it was almost undetectable.

Spandrell leaned over the couch in alarm. 'What's happening to him?'

Engin studied the row of dials on the console before him. 'Well, apparently it worked, Castellan. Only the Doctor's body is with us now. His mind has gone into the Matrix.'

The Doctor was lying against a rock in the middle of an enormous plain. From all around came booming, mad laughter, filling the skies like thunder.

He struggled to his feet and took a step forward. All at once there was a river before him. Out surged a giant crocodile, jaws gaping wide. The Doctor jumped back, his foot twisting beneath him—and tumbled over the edge of a precipice. He scrabbled for a hold, grabbing desperately at a projecting root. For a moment he hung over a colossal drop, the endless mad laughter booming in his ears.

Holding on with one hand, the Doctor whipped the scarf from his neck and looped it round an over-hanging tree. Grabbing both ends, he started hauling himself up.

A terrifying figure appeared on the cliff-top above him. Robed and masked, it carried an enormous sword. With no particular surprise, the Doctor recognised a Japanese Samurai warrior from the planet Earth.

The sword swept down cutting through the scarf, and the Doctor fell into endless space ...

7

Death by Terror

The Doctor's body lay motionless on the couch. Spandrell looked on helplessly, while Engin studied a monitor panel. Suddenly a steadily pulsing blip of light on the central gauge faded to nothingness. 'It's stopped,' said Engin sadly.

'What's stopped?'

'Brain activity.' Engin showed Spandrell the dial. 'Look, there's nothing registering.'

'Does that mean he's dead?'

The old Co-ordinator shrugged. 'Virtually. I warned him. The psychic shock of that environment ...'

Spandrell leaned over the Doctor's body. 'But he's still breathing—just about.'

Engin nodded. 'Motor activity. Often continues for some little time ... No, wait a minute ...' The blip had picked up. It was pulsing brightly. 'He's back! His brain must have an unusually high level of artron energy.'

The Doctor's chest was rising and falling, as his breathing became more regular. Spandrell looked down at him. 'What do you think's happening?'

Engin scanned his monitor dials. 'I don't know, Castellan. But whatever it is—to the Doctor it's completely and utterly real—real enough to kill him. If he dies in there—he'll die here too.'

The Doctor opened his eyes. He was stretched out on an operating table. Above him loomed the masked, gowned figure of a surgeon. There must have been an accident, thought the Doctor muzzily. He'd been hurt, and now he was in hospital. Yet there was something terribly wrong. Why was the operating table set up in the middle of an open plain? And why was the surgeon lunging at him with an enormous hypodermic?

'You were a fool, Doctor, to enter my domain,' shouted the surgeon.

In sudden panic, the Doctor rolled from the table. He hit hard, rocky ground, scrambled to his feet and started running . . .

He was on a battlefield, shells whistling all around him. A battle-weary soldier on an equally weary horse appeared out of the smoke and plodded towards him. Grotesquely, both soldier and horse were wearing gas masks. There was something sinister about them, a smell of death. The Doctor turned and fled . . .

He was running along a railway track. A masked guard loomed up before him, and pulled a heavy lever. The lines at the Doctor's feet shifted, as the points were changed. His foot was trapped between the rails. There was an express train roaring along the line towards him . . .

'No,' shouted the Doctor. 'No!' His foot came free —and the train roared past ...

... and he was stumbling over rocky ground. There was a sudden splintering crack. The Doctor looked down. He had stepped onto an enormous green egg. The case was shattered, and green liquid dripped from his foot. Somewhere in the distance there was a sniggering sound, like an evil child.

The Doctor made a mighty effort to concentrate his mind. He knew well enough what was happening to him. His adversary was attacking while he was still off-balance, trying to destroy him with all the traditional terrors—falling, illness, war, being trapped ... Unless the Doctor started fighting back, his enemy would hunt him down and kill him. Mental death, death by terror here in the Matrix, would mean physical death for the helpless body on the couch.

The Doctor stared hard at the plain around him. 'I deny this reality ... the true reality is a computation Matrix.'

The scene before him blurred—and turned into an endless vista of condensers and giant solid-state circuits. The Doctor knew his brain was perceiving the true nature of the Matrix that held it ... But the effort was too great, his enemy's reality too well established. The picture faded ...

This time he was at the bottom of a rocky quarry. It was unbearably hot. A vulture wheeled overhead in the coppery sky.

Doggedly the Doctor scrambled to his feet. He was

very thirsty, and he could hear water trickling ... It seemed to come from beneath a patch of damp sand. A hidden spring, perhaps ... The Doctor scraped away the sand to reveal not water, but a shining mirror. A clown's face leered up at him, and burst into a wild howl of laughter ... The vision faded, and the Doctor looked round; he was alone in the quarry. A voice boomed, '*I* am the creator here, Doctor. This is my world. There is no escape for you!' There was something oddly familiar about that voice, thought the Doctor, distorted though it was. He started climbing out of the quarry.

He was trudging across a dusty plain, beneath an ever-burning sun. Just ahead was a range of jungle-covered hills, with occasional outcrops of bare rock. There was a drone high above him. The Doctor looked up. An old-fashioned biplane was circling overhead. As the Doctor watched, the plane banked steeply, and dived straight towards him. He turned and ran. There was a staccato chattering and machine-gun bullets sprayed all round him. The Doctor saw a rocky gully and dived for it, rolling over and over, bullets tearing up the ground. His left leg felt suddenly numb ... The Doctor looked up. The plane was so low now that he could see the helmeted, goggled face of the pilot, laughing in triumph. The plane rose slowly and disappeared into the sky.

The Doctor looked at his leg. It was twisted at an awkward angle, and blood was seeping slowly through the cloth. 'I deny this reality,' he shouted. 'I deny it.'

The blood disappeared and his leg was whole again.

The voice from nowhere howled, 'You are trapped in my creation—and *my* reality rules here.'

The Doctor looked down. His leg was bleeding once more. 'All right,' muttered the Doctor grimly. 'Then I'll fight you in your reality—and on your own terms.' He tore a strip from his shirt and started bandaging his leg.

'It will be my pleasure to destroy you, Doctor,' threatened the voice. 'Be on guard!'

Engin studied his monitoring panel. The Doctor lay quite still on his couch, electrodes clamped to his head.

'His pulse has increased,' said Engin slowly. 'And there's a massive blood sugar demand.'

'What does that mean?'

'He's preparing to run—or to fight.'

'Then in that case,' asked Spandrell, '*who*, or *what*, is he fighting?'

'Presumably—another hostile mind.'

In the hidden chamber deep beneath the Capitol another A.P.C. set-up had been installed, secretly linked by the Master to the power-lines that fed the Matrix. The Time Lord who was now the Master's servant lay prone on a couch. The Master's bodily degeneration was too far advanced for him to undergo the physical strain involved in entering the Matrix. In any case, he had always preferred to find others to endure such risks. So it was the Time Lord whose mind was now inside the Matrix, the Time Lord who was risking life and sanity in an attempt to destroy the Doctor.

There was a flat plastic disc covering the Time Lord's face. It showed the Master what his servant was seeing, in the phantom world of the Matrix. At the moment it was little enough—a vista of heavy jungle, as the Time Lord's Matrix-self forced its way through the undergrowth.

The Master seemed well-satisfied. 'We have him now,' he hissed. 'But be wary. The Doctor is never more dangerous than when the odds are against him.'

A Chancellery Guard stood motionless in the corner. But his staring eyes saw nothing. He was under the Master's control, a mindless tool waiting to be used.

The Doctor finished bandaging his leg, and stood up to see if it would bear his weight. The leg was painful, and stiffening rapidly, but he could still walk. Ignoring the discomfort, he moved out of the rocks, and headed for the cover of the nearby jungle.

As soon as the Doctor was out of sight, the Hunter appeared. He wore dark jungle-green clothing, and his face was obscured by a jungle hat to which was fastened a camouflage net. He carried an elaborate telescopically-sighted rifle. His belt held a holstered pistol and a heavy knife. More equipment was packed into the light haversack on his back. Perfectly trained, fully equipped for jungle warfare, he was a formidable and terrifying figure.

Lightweight binoculars were slung round his neck,

and he was using them to scan the jungle ahead. Soon he froze, smiling in satisfaction. In the vision-field of the binoculars he could see the Doctor, working his way painfully up a rocky slope. The Doctor's trousers were torn, and his shirt was a tattered rag. He was tired, hungry and thirsty—and wounded. Above all, he was lost and confused in a world not of his making. The Hunter smiled. It wouldn't take long to finish so weak an opponent. He raised his rifle to his shoulder.

The Doctor had just paused for a much-needed rest when an explosive bullet blew a chunk from the rock beside his head. He rolled over and ran desperately for cover.

Scrambling to his feet, the Doctor burst through a dense clump of bushes, crossed a shallow valley and started climbing yet another rocky hill. Bullets buzzed about him like angry wasps. The Doctor reached the top of the hill and began a wild scramble down the other side. For the moment the hill itself shielded him from his pursuer. He looked round for a hiding place, and spotted a shallow cave. Scrambling inside, he pulled vegetation over the entrance to conceal himself, and crouched waiting.

From the back of the cave an enormous purple spider watched him from its web.

Belly-down on the ground, the Hunter crawled over the skyline, fearing that the Doctor would be waiting in ambush. Seeing nothing, he rose to his feet, and began descending the other side, rifle at the ready.

The Doctor crouched motionless in his cave as the booted feet came ever nearer.

The Hunter was only a few feet away from the

Doctor's hiding place. He looked round suspiciously, sensing that the Doctor was near, but unable to see him. He took the water bottle from his pack, and drank thirstily—and the act of drinking gave him an idea. 'That's it,' he whispered to himself. 'He'll need water soon. He'll have to come to water.'

Light as it was, the pack was slowing his movements. Slipping it from his shoulders, he hid it beneath a bush, then moved quietly away into the jungle.

A few minutes later, the Doctor crept out from his cave. He listened cautiously for a moment, then dragged out the Hunter's pack and started rummaging through it. Opening the water-bottle he lifted it eagerly to his lips—it was empty. He tossed it aside and started searching the pack. He found spare magazines, night-sights, plastic explosive, electric detonators, field rations, even a hand-grenade. 'Everything but an anti-tank gun,' muttered the Doctor morosely. He hefted the hand-grenade thoughtfully for a moment. Then he searched through the pack again, until he found a coil of very fine wire.

The Doctor chose a tree just beyond the bush, and higher up the hill. Carefully, he wedged the hand-grenade into the fork of one of its branches. He tied the wire round the pin of the grenade, then, unwinding the wire coil behind him, he moved back to the bush. Hurriedly re-packing the Hunter's haversack, he fastened the other end of the wire to a buckle, leaving just enough slack to allow him to thrust the knapsack back under the bush. Kicking dust and twigs over the length of the wire between bush and tree, the Doctor limped away into the jungle. The Hunter crouched by a jungle water hole, took a phial from his pocket and tipped it into the pool. An ugly green stain spread slowly over the surface of the water, gradually disappearing as the liquid dissolved. Tossing the phial to one side, the Hunter moved quietly away.

The Doctor came limping along the track, searching the jungle in his quest for water. Suddenly he paused. He could hear rustling. Then he relaxed—the sound was moving away from him. 'Wonder what he's been up to,' he thought, and moved cautiously on.

The Hunter ran back through the jungle to the place where he had left his haversack. He soon found the right bush, but the haversack seemed to be jammed. He tugged at it impatiently ...

The Hunter's tugging tightened the wire, which pulled the pin from the grenade, at the same time dislodging it from its tree-fork ...

Puzzled, the Hunter looked down at the haversack, and saw the wire fastened to the buckle. Immediately suspecting a trap he jumped to his feet—just in time to see the grenade rolling downhill towards him ...

With a shout of alarm the Hunter threw himself to one side, rolling over and over. The grenade exploded in a shattering blast of flame and smoke. Dust filled the air, and rock fragments rained down into the surrounding jungle.

Not far away, the Doctor was resting wearily against a tree. He lifted his head eagerly at the sound of the explosion, and as its echoes died away, he gazed hopefully around him. He saw only the familiar vista of hills and jungle. His head sunk despondently on his chest. 'Didn't get him after all ... if I had this nightmare would have vanished.' Rocks and jungle were only the creation of his enemy's mind. And since they were still here, his enemy still lived.

The Hunter picked himself up. He was dazed, dusty and wounded. Blood welled slowly from a gash in his side. Beneath the camouflage mask, his face was twisted in hate. 'A good try, Doctor. But not quite good enough!' Painfully he wriggled round, reached into his pack for an emergency dressing. He ripped open his jacket and started to bandage his wounds.

The Master straightened up with an angry snarl. 'The fool! To let himself be booby-trapped like that—the psychic shock might well have been fatal.' He studied the readings on his monitor dials. 'Physical condition worsening. If he doesn't finish the Doctor off soon ... he'll lose.'

The Master limped angrily about the room, cursing his physical deterioration. The trouble with working through others was that you were powerless to correct their bungling. He remembered the Guard sitting in the corner of the room, and came to a halt in front of him. A skeletal finger reached out to touch the Guard's forehead. 'Stand!'

The Guard rose and stood to attention, eyes glazed

and face blank. 'I have a task for you,' whispered the Master. 'There may be difficulties. Others may seek to prevent you from carrying out my orders. You will ignore them, and obey only me. You will let nothing stop you, do you understand?'

The Guard's voice was flat and emotionless. 'Yes, Master. I will obey only you.'

'Then this is what you must do ...' Hoarsely the Master gave a series of commands. The Guard marched away.

The Master's bloodless lips drew back in a smile of hatred. The body, as well as the mind, could be attacked. If the Master's plan worked, the struggle within the Matrix would soon be ended—by the Doctor's death ...

8

Duel to the Death

The Doctor broke into a shambling run at the sight
of the water hole. He was very thirsty now, and the
little pool of cool clear water seemed like some
wonderful mirage. But it was real enough—as real as
anything was here ... The Doctor flung himself down,
cupped his hands in the water and started to drink.

His lips were actually touching the water, when he
saw the dead fish floating just below the surface of the
pool. He paused, letting the water drain away between his hands, and looked deeper into the pool.
There was another dead fish—and another.

Slowly the Doctor straightened up, forcing himself
to move away from the water. He began a methodical
search of the area around the pool. Before very long,
he discovered the phial the Hunter had thrown away.
The Doctor took off the stopper and sniffed cautiously.
There were still a few drops of oily green liquid left
in the bottom. He stoppered the phial and slipped it
into his pocket. Perhaps he could find a way to turn
the enemy's weapon against him ...

There was a clump of bamboo growing near the
pool, and an idea came to him. He broke off first a
fairly thick bamboo cane and then a very thin one.
He found a flat rock and started digging a shallow

81

hole beside the little pool. When the hole was finished, the Doctor began using the thin cane to push the soft pith from the centre of the thick one. He worked with frantic speed. The Hunter couldn't be very far away.

By now the Hunter had finished dressing his wounds. He climbed stiffly to his feet, picked up his rifle and started moving back towards the water hole ...

A few inches of water had seeped into the bottom of the Doctor's hole. It came from the underground spring that fed the water hole itself—pure water uncontaminated by the Hunter's poison. Unable to wait any longer, the Doctor dipped his hollowed-out bamboo cane into the inch or two of muddy water and sucked greedily. Soon the water was gone. Some instinct told the Doctor there was no time to wait for more. He got to his feet, still clutching the bamboo cane, and moved off into the jungle.

The Hunter limped down the path to the water hole, rifle at the ready. He stood by the pool a moment, reading the Doctor's movements from his tracks. He saw the newly-dug mud-hole, and smiled. Water was only just seeping into the bottom again—which meant the Doctor wasn't far away.

He raised his voice in a taunting shout, 'I'm very close to you now, Doctor. You'd better start running...'

The Doctor was already running, forcing his way through the jungle. At the sound of the Hunter's voice he increased his pace—and blundered straight into a clump of thorn-trees. He tried to tear himself free but the thorns were long and sharp, tearing savagely at his clothing, and at his flesh.

The Hunter heard the crackling, smiled in satisfaction, and set off at a run.

The Doctor forced himself to move slowly and patiently, unhooking the tangling thorns one by one. As the last thorn came free, he could hear the Hunter crashing through the jungle.

The Doctor looked round wildly, and a desperate plan formed in his mind. He snapped off several of the longest thorns, and headed for a huge gnarled tree that grew nearby. Bamboo cane in one hand, he grabbed one of the lower branches and began hauling himself painfully upwards, handicapped by his tiredness, and the pain from his wounded leg.

Finally he reached his objective, a broad high branch which overhung the jungle floor. Sprawled on top of it, the Doctor fished out the phial and one of the thorns. He dipped the point of the thorn into the drops of green liquid in the phial. Then he slipped the treated thorn into one end of his hollow bamboo cane—and waited.

The Hunter appeared below him, limping stiffly through the jungle. Like the Doctor, he was ragged and exhausted. But it was clear from the way he held the high-powered rifle that every sense was on the alert.

The Doctor watched him pass beneath the tree,

raised his improvised blow-pipe to his lips and *blew*.

The second he felt the sting of the thorn the Hunter whirled round and fired. Shot like a roosting bird, the Doctor tumbled from his tree and crashed down into the undergrowth. clutching his arm.

The Hunter moved to finish him off—and became aware of a spreading numbness ... He looked down and saw the thorn projecting from his thigh. Gritting his teeth he plucked it out. His face paled at the sight of the green stain on its tip. He had minutes to live—unless ...

Throwing the thorn aside, he began hunting frantically through his pockets. With a sigh of relief, he found a pocket medi-kit, opened the little case and took out an injector-phial of antidote. Quickly he plunged the injector-needle into the muscle above the wound.

The Doctor staggered to his feet, his wounded arm hanging limply by his side. He looked round at the absorbed Hunter and realised he had only a few moments to escape. Gathering the remnants of his strength, the Doctor reeled off into the cover of the jungle.

A Chancellery Guard marched stiffly into the Records Section and came to attention before Spandrell.

'Message from the Chancellor, sir. He wants the Doctor brought to him for interrogation.'

'You're Solis, aren't you? One of the Chancellor's personal bodyguard.'

'That's right, sir.'

'Well, whoever he is, he will have to wait,' said Engin peevishly. 'I can't just snatch the Doctor's mind out of the Matrix. The shock would kill him.'

'You mean we can't get him out?' asked Spandrell. 'What *do* we do then?'

'Wait till he comes back of his own accord—*if* he does. When the mind is back in the body, the body can be disconnected from the machine—and not before.'

Spandrell waved the Guard to one side. 'You heard the Co-ordinator. The Chancellor can't interrogate a corpse. You'll have to wait.'

Solis nodded silently, and took up a position close to the monitor console.

Spandrell turned back to Engin. 'How long can a living mind exist in there?'

'I've no idea. There's just no data available. But I can tell you this—his body's on the point of collapse.' Engin pointed towards the monitor console. 'Low blood pressure, shallow respiration ... He can't go on much longer.'

Solis was studying the area around the couch. The various electrodes connecting the Doctor to the machine all came together at one main point. If those wires were wrenched free, the Doctor would die from the shock—and Solis would have carried out his mission.

Very slowly he began edging nearer to the console.

The Doctor staggered on through the jungle, too weak to think of fighting. The one idea in his mind was to

85

survive. Somehow he must outlast his terrible enemy. 'Must keep going,' he muttered. 'I *must* keep going.'

He stumbled and fell, and lay gasping, feeling as if he could never move again. Then he struggled slowly to his feet and staggered on. *'I must keep going...'*

Ahead of him the jungle was thinning out. Beyond it there was a misty swamp bordering a stagnant palm-fringed lagoon. The Doctor stumbled on towards the water.

Following close behind, the Hunter was almost as exhausted as his quarry. His side throbbed dully, and even after the antidote, the poisoned thorn had left his right leg feeling numb and heavy. But like the Doctor, he was utterly determined not to give up.

He reached the spot where the Doctor had fallen, and examined the place where the Doctor's body had rested. The Hunter fingered a blade of blood-stained grass. 'He can't last much longer,' he muttered. 'He *can't*.' The hoarse whisper was almost a prayer. The Hunter knew he couldn't last much longer himself.

'It's only a *mental* battle they're fighting,' said Spandrell angrily. 'If the Doctor is losing, why doesn't he just pull out?'

'It isn't that simple. His adversary must have been in the Matrix many times before. He's created a kind of mental landscape—a *dreamscape* if you like. The Doctor's caught up in it ...' Engin noticed a flicker of movement beside him, and turned to see Solis stretching a hand towards the nexus of electrode wires.

'Don't touch, you fool! Do you want to kill him?'

'Sorry sir. Just curious.' Solis moved back—but not very far.

'If the Doctor is trapped in his enemy's world,' insisted Spandrell, 'then the enemy is bound to be stronger. The Doctor doesn't stand a chance.'

'Well, perhaps a very slight one.' Engin looked up from the monitor dials. 'You see, Castellan, the Doctor's opponent is expending energy in the very act of maintaining the reality-projection he has created. The Doctor, on the other hand, is free to employ all his mental energy for self-defence.'

Solis had edged closer by now. He stretched out a stealthy hand towards the clump of wires. By the time Spandrell registered the stealthy movement, it was almost too late. 'Get back,' he roared. 'Get back!'

Solis lunged forward. As his finger-tips touched the wires Spandrell drew his staser and fired all in one smooth motion. Solis was hurled back by the massive shock of the staser-bolt. He should have collapsed at once but so strong was the Master's hypnotic command that the dying body lurched forward in an attempt to carry out its mission. Horrified, Spandrell fired again, and again, and the body jerked and lay still.

Slowly, Spandrell holstered his staser as frightened attendants came running from all sides. Engin looked at the Doctor, stretched immobile on the couch, then studied the monitor dials. 'He's calling on all his reserves,' he whispered. 'The final struggle is about to begin!'

Entering the marsh had been a bad mistake, thought

the Doctor. True he had been able to drink from the lagoon, and the brackish water had made him feel stronger. But the ground was soft and boggy now and progress was very slow. He pulled a long straight branch from a fallen tree, stripped it into a staff and used it to feel his way along. He had no wish to be trapped sinking in a swamp when the Hunter caught up with him. Would his enemy haul him out for the pleasure of shooting him, wondered the Doctor? Or would he simply sit and watch him disappear slowly beneath the mud?

Just ahead of him was an area of scattered shallow mud-pools. From time to time one or another of them produced a sudden pop. 'Marsh gas,' thought the Doctor. He sniffed. 'Smells like methane ...'

Just beyond the pools was a clump of bushes. The Doctor limped slowly towards it. He burrowed deep beneath the shelter of the broad leaves and slid forward onto his face, head pillowed in his arms. The loss of blood from his wounds, and the arduous journey through jungle and swamp had been too much for him. He was utterly exhausted.

So too was the Hunter. He was lurching wearily through the swamp, stumbling blindly on, his eyes glazed with fatigue. The swampy landscape seemed to dissolve and swim about him, as if the world of his creation was about to disappear.

The Hunter's exhaustion was registered on the

monitor panels in the underground chamber where his real, physical body still lay. The Master hovered angrily over the unconscious form of his champion. 'Come, one final effort. Kill the Doctor. Destroy him. I, the Master, command you!'

The Hunter straightened up, like a puppet when its operator tightens the strings. Once more, fresh and alert, he gazed keenly round the swamps and picked up the clear tracks leading to the Doctor's hiding place.

Picking his way towards the bubbling pools, he shouted, 'Where are you, Doctor? You can't win now—you might as well give up!'

Wearily the Doctor raised his head. Parting the leaves, he saw the Hunter advancing towards him, rifle at the ready.

The Doctor wriggled backwards, into deeper cover. 'What do you want?'

The Hunter's voice rang back. 'Only your life, Doctor ...' There was a peal of hideous laughter. 'Only your life, for my Master!'

'I'll make a bargain with you!'

'No bargains. Show yourself, Doctor. Get it over with. Do you hear me?'

The Doctor was working his way to the far edge of the clump of swamp-bushes. 'No!' he shouted. 'You show yourself, first. Your *real* self.'

'Very well, Doctor.' The Hunter snatched off his mask and for the first time the Doctor saw the face of his enemy. It was Chancellor Goth.

The Doctor sighed wearily. How like the Master to corrupt the highest and the noblest of the Time Lords to his evil purposes. 'All right, Goth,' he called. 'You win. I'm coming out.'

Holding his long pole by one end he slid it along the ground to its full extent, until it lodged against a bush as far away from him as he could reach. Watching the mud-pools, the Doctor chose his moment, then shoved hard.

Goth saw the movement of the bushes, swung up his rifle and fired—just as the nearest pool sent up a puff of inflammable marsh-gas.

The explosive bullet touched off the marsh-gas, and flames sprang up all around. Suddenly Goth was trapped in a ring of fire. His clothes caught fire and with a roar of pain he flung down his rifle and dashed madly towards the lagoon.

As he got to his feet and came out of the bushes the Doctor was just in time to see Goth plunge into the water and disappear.

Retrieving his pole, the Doctor ran after him. He must finish his enemy while he was weak—then his nightmare world would be finished too.

By the time the Doctor reached the lagoon, Goth was nowhere in sight. The dark, stagnant water was completely still. The Doctor waded in waist-deep, probing the water with his pole. This world was still in existence—which meant that somewhere Goth was still alive.

The water behind him exploded in spray, as Goth surfaced with the savage fury of an attacking shark. The Doctor tried to turn, but Goth was too quick for him. Gripping him savagely round the neck, Goth bore the Doctor down and down until his head was beneath the water. The Doctor flailed and struggled, sending up great clouds of spray. But Goth had a grip of iron. He thrust the Doctor down and down until his head was under water.

The Doctor kicked and struggled for a moment longer. Then suddenly his body went limp ...

'You're finished, Doctor,' snarled Goth. 'Finished!'

9

The End of Evil

Goth held the Doctor under water a moment longer, then relaxed his grip on the limp body. Suddenly the Doctor came to life, catapulting up and backwards, knocking Goth off his feet. As Goth disappeared under the water the Doctor raised his long pole and speared downwards, pinning Goth's body to the muddy bed of the lagoon.

There was frantic kicking and thrashing and bubbling as Goth churned up the water in his efforts to escape. Grimly, the Doctor bore down on the pole, using the last vestiges of his strength to hold Goth under . . .

. . . and Goth's body vanished. The lagoon itself vanished, and the swamps and jungles around it.

The Doctor saw an endless vista of solid-state circuitry stretching ahead of him. Pretending to risk his champion's death rather than his defeat, the Master had snatched Goth out of the Matrix.

On the couch Goth's body thrashed and convulsed. Angrily the Master slammed down switches on his control console. 'You weak fool! You craven-hearted, spineless poltroon, you let the Doctor trick you. You have failed me!'

'He was too strong for me, Master ... too much mental energy.'

The Master was busy at his console setting up new circuits. Goth, too weak to move, watched him with alarm. 'What are you doing, Master?'

'There's only one chance now. I must trap him in the Matrix forever. I shall overload the neuron fields ...'

'No, Master, no!' screamed Goth. 'For pity's sake take off these connections. You'll kill me!'

The Master shook his head. It would be a long and complex job to disconnect Goth from the machine without harming him—and every second was precious. 'I've no time to waste on you,' he muttered, and pulled the switch. Goth's body arched in pain as the connections burned out. As the final blackness swallowed him, Goth saw the face of the Master staring down at him. It was the twisted, malformed face of a decaying corpse ...

A series of explosions shook Engin's console, and smoke poured from the burnt-out connections. Engin reached for the main power switch in panic, but Spandrell grabbed his arm. 'Co-ordinator, you can't. If you cut the power, the Doctor will die in there.'

'The circuits are going. If there's a fire in there the whole panoptric net will burn out. Thousands of brain patterns destroyed for ever.'

'They're not alive,' said Spandrell brutally. 'The Doctor is—I hope!'

The Doctor was fleeing across a darkening plain. The sky was blazing, and there were shattering explosions all around him. The ground erupted in flames, and the Doctor realised it was useless to run. He stared unafraid at the devastated landscape. 'I deny this reality,' he shouted. 'Goth has gone—and his world must vanish too!' There was another tremendous explosion. The Doctor vanished into a cloud of choking yellow smoke ...

... and woke coughing on the couch in the Records Section. 'Do you mind,' he murmured, 'this is a non-smoking compartment!' He realised he was rambling, opened his eyes, and saw Spandrell staring down at him.

Engin looked up from his monitor console. 'It's all right, Castellan,' he called. 'He's made it!' He threw the main switch to cut the power. Then he went over to the Doctor, and began to remove the electrodes.

The Master cursed, as a warning light on his own console blinked out. 'They've cut the power to the panotropic net! The Doctor must have eluded me.'

Goth stirred feebly on the couch, feeling life ebb from his burnt-out body. 'You fiend,' he whispered. 'Why did I ever believe in you ...' His head fell back.

The Master ignored him, his mind racing. He knew the Doctor would soon be on his track. His decaying body was too infirm to endure a long chase. He might not even reach his TARDIS. Were Spandrell's Guards to hunt him through the Capitol like a dying rat? No! Not while there was a better way. He took a gleaming hypodermic from beneath his robe, pushed back his sleeve, and plunged the needle into the vein of one skeletal arm.

Spandrell helped the Doctor to sit up. 'How do you feel?'

'Tired,' said the Doctor. 'Very, very tired.' He tried to stand and staggered a little.

Spandrell helped him to sit down again. 'You'd better rest, Doctor. You took a terrible beating in there.'

The Doctor grinned. 'You should see the other fellow. Where is he, by the way?'

'Where's who?'

'Goth! We've got to find him. He's your assassin, Spandrell. He's been acting as the Master's leg man.'

'Goth,' said Spandrell slowly. 'So that's why he was so keen to have you executed.'

The Doctor made a mighty effort, and actually managed to get onto his feet. 'Exactly. It was Goth, remember, who ordered my TARDIS to be transducted to the Capitol ... He knew very well I was still in it. He just wanted to make sure I was in the right place at the right time.'

The Doctor tried a few tentative steps, as he felt

his strength returning. 'Goth and the Master must have set up their own private link into the Matrix, so they can't be very far away. We can use the link to trace them.' He came to a stop in front of the bemused Engin. 'What's below us here?'

'Below the tower itself? Only service ducts . . .'

'And below them?'

'Well, a long way down there are vaults and tunnels dating back to the old time. They were never destroyed, simply built over . . . There's an old map somewhere . . .'

Now almost himself again, the Doctor said impatiently, 'Fetch it! Come on, what are you waiting for?' He bustled Engin away. Spandrell lifted his communicator. If they were going to hunt for the Master, he wanted some Guards at his back. No one was going to turn him into a miniaturised corpse.

It didn't take very long to find the Master's secret hiding place. Using Engin's map, the Doctor worked out the most likely points for the Master to have tapped the Matrix power lines, and then checked them one by one.

The search led far below the city, along dank echoing stone corridors and into musty vaults disused for hundreds of years. At last they found what they were looking for—at the bottom of a long flight of time-worn steps, there was a tiny stone-walled chamber. As soon as the Doctor entered it, he knew their search was over.

In one corner was an incongruous clutter of technological equipment ... the Master's monitor console, the power cables linking it to the Matrix. Goth's unconscious body was slumped back on the couch, just barely breathing.

Dominating the little room was a high-backed stone chair. In it sat a cowled figure, motionless as a statue. The Doctor went slowly up to it, and pushed back the cowl.

Spandrell was close behind him, blaster in hand. He recoiled at the sight of the ravaged face beneath the hood. 'Is it him, Doctor?'

The Doctor nodded. 'Yes ... it's the Master.' The Master's head lolled backwards. The eyes in the skull-like face stared sightlessly at the ceiling. With some distaste, Spandrell felt for a pulse in the skinny wrist. There was nothing. He let go of the wrist with relief. 'He's dead, right enough.'

Engin was examining Goth. 'The Chancellor's still alive ... barely.'

They moved to the couch, and Spandrell looked down at Goth. 'Not for long though, by the looks of him.'

Engin was disconnecting terminals from the Chancellor's body. 'He seems to have taken the full blast of power from the Matrix.'

Goth opened his eyes and looked up at the Doctor. 'So, Doctor. You beat us in the end.'

'Goth,' said the Doctor sadly. 'Why did you do it?'

'I wanted *power* ...' whispered the dying voice.

'You would have been President ...'

'No ...' gasped Goth painfully. 'The retiring President told me ... wasn't going to name me his successor. Thought I was too ambitious ...'

'So you killed him.'

Goth gestured weakly towards the motionless figure in the chair.

'I killed for *him*. The Master ... part of his plan ... doomsday plan ...'

The Doctor leaned forward. '*What* plan, Goth?'

Goth paused for a moment, then spoke with a last tremendous effort. 'I discovered him in hiding, on Tersurus ... He was already dying. No more regenerations ... He promised me power ... made me bring him to Gallifrey, and hide him down here ...' Goth closed his eyes.

The Doctor said urgently. 'Goth, you've got to tell us ... what was this doomsday plan?'

Spandrell pulled him away. 'It's no use, Doctor. He's dead.'

The Doctor glared down angrily at the body. 'Typical politician—they'll never give you a straight answer to a straight question.'

Spandrell looked at him in astonishment. Then suddenly he understood. Beneath his flippant manner, the Doctor was very worried.

Some time later, they were all in the Chancellery, explaining the astonishing sequence of events to Cardinal Borusa. The sudden death of both President and Chancellor had left the old Cardinal as the leader of the High Council. He was quite prepared to take over both offices until the crisis was over.

Despite the lateness of the hour, Borusa was still

fresh and alert, and he listened keenly as Spandrell concluded his account of the Chancellor's death. 'Apparently the Master tried to trap the Doctor in the Matrix by overloading the neuron fields, leaving Chancellor Goth still connected to the circuit. The shock killed him.'

'And the Master's own death?'

Spandrell shrugged. 'You might almost say natural causes, sir. The body was extremely decayed. It's a wonder he stayed alive so long. One can only presume that he had come to the end of his regeneration cycle prematurely.'

Borusa frowned. 'I understood he was relatively young—not much older than the Doctor here.'

The Doctor was standing by the window, brooding over the lights of the Capitol City far below. 'He was always a criminal, sir, throughout all his lives. Constant pressure, constant danger. Accelerated regenerations used as disguise ... He was simply burnt out.'

Borusa nodded sombrely. Time Lord regeneration was a delicate and complex business. When something did go wrong with it, the results were often catastrophic.

The old Cardinal sat brooding behind the huge ornate desk that had once belonged to Goth. Suddenly he stood up. 'No!' he said decisively.

The Doctor gave him a puzzled look. 'No, what?'

'This wild story. It's unacceptable.'

'It happens to be the truth.'

'Then we must adjust the truth!'

'Adjust it, Cardinal?' Engin was shocked. 'In what way?'

'In a way that will maintain confidence in the Time Lords, and in their leadership. How many people have seen Goth and the Master since their deaths?'

Spandrell considered. 'Apart from those of us in this room? Just Hildred and the Guards.'

'We can rely on their silence.' Borusa thought for a moment. 'Castellan, you will see that the appearance of the Master's body is altered. We all know the effects of a staser-bolt. It will be a simple matter to char the body beyond recognition.'

'For what purpose, Cardinal?'

Borusa looked round the circle of puzzled faces. 'The official story will be that the Master arrived secretly on Gallifrey, and assassinated the President. Before he could escape, Chancellor Goth tracked him down and killed him, unfortunately perishing himself in an exchange of staser fire.' Borusa gave a wintry smile. 'Now, that's a much better story. I can believe that.'

Engin was appalled. 'After all that happened, you're going to make *Goth* into a hero?'

'The people need heroes, Co-ordinator. Sometimes it's even necessary to invent them. Good for public morale.'

'And what of the Doctor's part in all this?' asked Spandrell.

'Best forgotten,' said Borusa briskly. 'Naturally, Doctor, all charges against you will be dropped.'

The Doctor gave a mock bow. 'How very kind.'

'Providing, of course, that you leave Gallifrey at once.'

'Somehow, Cardinal, I have no desire to stay.'

'Good. Now, I believe you know something of the Master's past?'

'We did bump into each other from time to time.'

'Before you leave you will assist Co-ordinator Engin to compile a new biography of him—to replace the one that was stolen. It needn't be entirely accurate, of course.'

'Like Time Lord history?'

Borusa ignored the jibe. 'A few facts will give it verisimilitude, Co-ordinator. We cannot make the Master into a public enemy if we know nothing about him.'

Engin bowed his head. 'If that is your order, Cardinal, I can have a new biography prepared by morning.'

'I leave it to you. Later I think we must hold a thorough review of data security. We cannot have Time Lord data extracts simply vanishing from the records.'

Spandrell accepted the implied rebuke. 'I quite agree, sir. I'll see procedures are tightened up.'

'You'll attend to the, er, cosmetic treatment.'

'I'm sorry, Cardinal?'

'The alteration in the appearance of the Master's body,' said Borusa impatiently.

'I'll give orders immediately.'

'Excellent. I think that's all, gentlemen.' With a brief nod of farewell, Cardinal Borusa strode from the room.

A little sadly, the Doctor watched him go. 'Only in

mathematics will you find the truth,' he murmured to himself.

Engin stared at him. 'What was that, Doctor?'

'Something Borusa used to say, during my time at the Academy. Now he's trying to prove it.'

In accordance with Spandrell's orders, Hildred and the Guards were searching the Master's hiding place. One of them found an empty hypodermic under the Master's chair. He passed it over to Hildred, whose wrist-communicator bleeped as he took it. Spandrell's face appeared in the tiny screen. 'Hildred? A little job for you. Don't worry, it's well within your capability.'

'Yes, Castellan.'

Spandrell hesitated. 'I'd better explain in person. Come to the Chancellery.'

'Immediately, Castellan.'

Slipping the empty hypodermic into his pocket, Hildred hurried from the room.

The black-robed body of the Master still sat upright in its high-backed chair. One of the Guards looked at it then turned away, with a shudder. The Master's bloodless lips seemed to have frozen in the trace of a smile...

10

The Doomsday Plan

The Doctor was comfortably sprawled in Engin's chair. The Co-ordinator himself sat at a nearby data terminal, attempting to feed details of the Master's disreputable career into the computer. He was getting very little help from the Doctor, who was gazing abstractedly into space.

'Now then, Doctor,' said Engin hopefully. 'What about the Master's *character*?'

'*Bad,*' said the Doctor.

Engin sighed. 'If you could possibly be a *little* more specific?'

'All right. Evil. Cunning. Resourceful. Determined. Technologically brilliant. Highly developed powers of extrasensory-perception. A remarkable hynotist ...' The Doctor broke off the list. 'You know, Engin, the more I think about him, the more unlikely it all becomes.'

'What does?'

'That the Master would meekly accept death. It's not his style.'

'Death is something we must all accept in time, Doctor,' said the old Time Lord gently.

'*Not the Master*. That must be why he came back here to Gallifrey. He had some plan.'

Obstinately Engin said. 'If the Master had triggered the end of his regeneration cycle, no plan could postpone his death.'

'You're certain of that? Surely in *theory* ...'

'In theory, perhaps, Doctor. But in practice, any attempt to *renew* the regeneration cycle would call for colossal amounts of energy.'

'How colossal?'

'Oh, say, about as much as we use to power the time travel facility. In other words the power of the whole of Gallifrey.' Engin smiled tolerantly, confident he'd disposed of the Doctor's nonsensical theory. 'Besides, why concern yourself further with the Master's evil schemes? He's dead now.'

'How do we know his doomsday plan isn't already under way? He may have had other servants as well as Goth. His evil scheme may be ticking away like a time bomb at this very moment.'

The Doctor jumped up and began pacing restlessly up and down. 'So then ... Something to do with energy, and something connected with Goth becoming President.' He swung round. 'What's so special about the President, Engin?'

'Nothing. He's simply a Time Lord, usually of senior rank, elected to a position of formal authority. He holds the ancient symbols of office, of course ...'

'Symbols? What symbols?'

'Relics from the Old Time. The Sash of Rassilon, the Great Key ...'

The Doctor stopped his pacing about, and dropped back into Engin's chair. 'Tell me about Rassilon, Co-ordinator.'

Engin brightened. Ancient History was a pet subject of his, and he was always glad of any opportunity to discuss it. 'Well, it's all recorded in the Book of Old Time. But there is a modern transgram of the text—that's much less difficult ...'

'Could I hear it?'

'You mean—*now*?'

'Now,' said the Doctor firmly.

Engin gave a resigned sigh, and got slowly to his feet. Suddenly he saw that the Doctor was sitting bolt upright, an expression of keen attention on his face. 'What is it, Doctor?'

'I can hear my hair curling,' said the Doctor solemnly, and grinned. 'Either I'm on the track of something—or it's going to rain!'

In a Chancellery office, Spandrell was giving Hildred instructions. 'Now have you got everything clear, Commander?'

'Yes, Castellan.'

Spandrell regarded him dubiously. 'You know why I chose you for this special mission, Commander Hildred?'

'No, Castellan.'

'Because the Master is already dead—which means that even you aren't likely to miss the target.'

'No, sir,' said Hildred patiently. He could see it was going to be a long time before Spandrell let him forget the way the Doctor had tricked him, when he'd first arrived on Gallifrey. Hildred saluted and turned to leave. Then he paused, taking the empty hypodermic from his pocket. 'Castellan, we found this ... under the Master's chair.'

Spandrell examined the hypodermic. 'Empty ... There'll probably be enough traces of the drug to analyse, though. Thank you, Commander. Report back to me when you've—restructured the Master.'

Co-ordinator Engin was happily lecturing the Doctor on his favourite subject. 'You see, Doctor, today we think of Rassilon as an almost mythical hero, the legendary founder of our Time Lord civilisation. But in his own time, he was regarded principally as a cosmic engineer. This of course was before we turned aside from the barren road of pure technology ...'

'That's very interesting,' said the Doctor patiently. 'Could we hear some more of the transgram, do you think?'

Engin adjusted controls on the playback console before him. 'Now let me see, this should be the area you're interested in ...' He touched a control, and a clear, melodic voice came from the console. 'And Rassilon journeyed into the black void with a great fleet. Within the Void no light would shine, and nothing of that outer nature could continue in being, save that which existed within the Sash of Rassilon.'

'A Black Hole,' muttered the Doctor excitedly. 'That's what it means—it must be!'

The melodic voice went on. 'Now Rassilon created the Eye of Harmony, which balances all things so that they neither flux nor wither nor change their state in any measure. And in this Eye, he sealed the energies of the Void with the Great Key, and caused the Eye of Harmony to be brought to Gallifrey ...'

'What is the Great Key, Engin? You mentioned it before.'

Engin switched off the transgram. 'It's just a plain black rod ... it looks like ebonite. The President carries it on certain ceremonial occasions, but its original function is a complete mystery.'

'Where is it kept, when it is not in use?'

'In the Panopticon. There's a special display section of relics from the Old Time.'

'And the Sash of Rassilon?'

'Oh, that stays with the President. The tradition is that it must always be in his possession. In fact it is the actual handing over of the Sash that signifies the transfer of the Presidency from one Time Lord to another ...'

The Doctor wasn't listening. 'Of course—that must be it. What a stupendous egotist.'

'Who?'

'The Master, of course. Don't you see? The Eye of Harmony is the inexhaustible energy source that powers all Gallifrey. It was that energy which made possible the first experiments in time travel. It's the whole source and foundation of Time Lord power, taken for granted for thousands of years ... and the Master planned to steal it. He'd have destroyed Gallifrey, the Time Lords, *everything*—just for the sake of his own survival!'

Spandrell came towards them, the Master's empty hypodermic in his hand. 'It seems that the Master didn't die of natural causes after all, Doctor. Apparently he killed himself.'

The Doctor frowned. 'That's even *less* like him.' He took the hypodermic, broke it open and sniffed delicately.

'I'd be careful, Doctor. Presumably it's some deadly poison!'

'Tricophenylaldehyde!' said the Doctor triumphantly.

Spandrell was none the wiser. 'It produces instant death, no doubt?'

'It produces the *appearance* of death. It's a neural inhibitor.'

'*What?*'

'He's fooled us, Spandrell. *The Master is still alive!*'

Spandrell looked at him in sudden dismay. 'I've just sent Hildred to blast the Master's body with a staser-bolt.'

'Where?'

'The Panopticon vault ...'

In a gloomy shadowed vault beneath the Panopticon, three bodies lay at rest on their marble biers. First the President, still in his ceremonial robes, the wide metallic links of the Sash of Rassilon draped across the dead chest. Next Goth, his handsome face cold and still. And finally the Master, still shrouded in black robe and cowl.

Feet rang on the flagstones and Commander Hildred came into the vault. He looked at the three still forms and shuddered. For all Spandrell's jest, it wasn't so easy to shoot a man who was already dead.

Bracing himself, Hildred crossed to the Master's bier. He drew and cocked his staser-pistol, holding it to the ghastly skull-like head. The Master's eyes opened. They blazed with malevolent hypnotic power, and Hildred found that he couldn't move. A skinny hand reached out and took him by the throat ...

As Hildred's body sank slowly to the stone floor, the Master sat up, swinging his legs from the marble slab. From beneath his robe he produced a squat, oddly-shaped gun ...

Spandrell, Engin and the Doctor hurried along the gloomy corridors of the Panopticon. The Doctor had a premonition that they were already too late ...

When the Master heard the sound of approaching footsteps, he moved away from the President's body wrapped himself in the black cloak, and stepped back into the shadows. Seconds later, Spandrell appeared in the doorway. Hildred was nowhere to be seen— and the bier which had held the Master was empty. Spandrell turned as the Doctor and Engin came up. 'We're too late, Doctor. He's gone.'

As Spandrell walked forward to the Master's bier, his foot struck something soft beneath it. He looked down, and saw the dead body of Hildred, shrunken to the size of a doll.

The Doctor looked down at the wizened corpse.

'The Master is consumed by hatred. It's his one great weakness.'

'Weakness, Doctor?' croaked a rasping voice. They turned to see the Master emerging from the shadows, Hildred's staser-pistol in his claw-like hand. 'That's where you're wrong. Hatred is strength.'

The Doctor said calmly, 'Not in your case. You'd delay an execution while you pulled the wings off a fly.'

'This time, I assure you, Doctor, the execution will not be delayed. *Don't!*' The Master's staser swung round to cover Spandrell, who had been edging a hand towards his pistol. 'I assure you, Castellan, I am not nearly so infirm as I look.' Spandrell stood very still, and the Master waved the staser at Engin. 'You! Bring the Sash of Rassilon.'

Engin looked at the Doctor. 'It appears you were right, Doctor.'

'Why else do you think I feigned death?' sneered the Master. 'When Goth failed me it was necessary to use more direct means. The Sash is wasted on a dead President, don't you think? *Bring it to me!*'

'Engin, don't do it,' said the Doctor quietly.

The ruined face turned towards him. 'I have suffered enough from your stupid interference in my designs, Doctor. Now we are coming to the end of our conflict and the victory is mine!'

'Why did you bring me here?' asked the Doctor quietly.

The Master smiled. 'As a scapegoat for the killing of the President, Doctor. Who else but you, so despicably good, so insufferably compassionate. I wanted you to die in shame and disgrace, destroyed by your own people, as I shall destroy them.'

Spandrell took advantage of the Master's speech to make his move. He sprang forward, snatching at his staser. Instantly, the Master shot him down. At the same time the Doctor sprang—and the Master scuttled quickly to one side and fired again. The Doctor's body joined Spandrell's on the ground. The staser swung round to cover Engin. 'Now—bring me the Sash, you old fool, or you'll get the same!'

Too terrified to refuse, Engin lifted the Sash from the body of the President, and handed it over. The Master snatched it, then hurried to the door of the vault. He looked back at the frightened Co-ordinator. 'Don't worry, I'm not going to kill you. Your friends aren't dead either—only stunned. I want you all to live long enough to see the end of this accursed planet —and for the Doctor to taste the full bitterness of his defeat.'

The Master slipped through the doorway, and an iron security shutter crashed down behind him. Engin heard a groaning sound. The Doctor was struggling to sit up. Spandrell too was beginning to stir.

With Engin's help, the Doctor struggled to his feet. 'The Sash? What happened to it?'

'I'm afraid it's gone, Doctor. What could I do? After all it's only of symbolic value.'

The Doctor groaned. 'Didn't you understand any-thing I was telling you? That Sash is a technological miracle, a device to enable the wearer to tap the power of the Eye of Harmony. All the Master needs now is the Great Key, and he can draw upon a force capable of obliterating this entire planet.'

Engin was stunned. 'You can't mean that, Doctor?'

'Of course I mean it! Don't you realise what Rassilon did—what the Eye of Harmony *is*? "That which balances all things", remember. It can only be one thing—the nucleus of a Black Hole.'

'But surely the Eye of Harmony is only a myth?'

'A myth? All the power of the Time Lords devolves from it.' Again the Doctor quoted from the transgram. ' "Neither flux nor wither nor change their state ..." Somehow Rassilon stabilised the elements of a Black Hole and set them in an eternally dynamic equation balanced against the mass of this planet. To get the energy he needs, the Master means to upset that balance by stealing the Eye. It will mean the end of Gallifrey, and it could set off an anti-matter chain reaction that will end hundreds of worlds.'

Spandrell climbed painfully to his feet. 'A very interesting exposition, Doctor. Now what are we going to do about it?'

The Doctor went to the shutter and heaved with all his strength. Spandrell and Engin tried to help— but the shutter was immovable. They were trapped in the vault. Trapped with a dead President and a dead Chancellor—and the Master was free.

11

The Final Battle

Black cloak almost invisible in the darkness of the Panopticon Museum, the Master crossed to the display case where the Great Key rested on its velvet cushion. Melting the lock with a blast from his staser-pistol, he lifted the glass dome and snatched up the gleaming black rod.

Swiftly he made his way into the main hall and up on to the platform. In the exact centre, he found a metal plate, worn smooth by the feet of generations of incurious Time Lords. The Master touched the plate with the black rod. It slid aside, to reveal a hole—the lock to which the black rod was the key. He slid the tip of the rod into the hole and turned it. There was a click, and a hum of power. There followed a whole series of clicks, as the Master turned the Key first one way and then the other, like someone manipulating a particularly intricate combination lock. With each series of turns the black rod slid further into the hole, until with a final click it disappeared completely. The Master scurried back, as the whole central area of the dais slid away, and a strange shape emerged ... It was a shining monolith, a pillar almost as tall as a man. It might have been carved from one enormous black diamond. The pillar was throbbing with unimaginable power. Six gleaming metallic coils ran from its base, and disappeared into the depths from which it had emerged.

The Master looked at the monolith. Even he was awed. 'Rassilon's Star!' he murmured. 'The Eye of Harmony...'

The Doctor and Spandrell were leaning exhausted by the vault door. They had heaved at the iron shutter until their muscles creaked, but nothing happened.

'It's no use,' said Engin despairingly. 'You'll never shift it!'

The Doctor straightened up and prowled restlessly around the vault. 'We've got to get out...' He paused by the far corner, and looked up. 'There's some kind of shaft over here... and a gleam of light at the top. Where does it lead?'

Spandrell peered upwards. 'To the Panopticon, I imagine. Looks like an old service shaft.'

'If you can get me into it, I can chimney myself up to the top.'

Engin looked up in horror. 'It's a hundred feet high, at least, Doctor. If you slip...'

The Doctor ignored him. 'Come on, Spandrell. If we drag the empty bier over to this corner... You get on, and I'll stand on your shoulders...' A faint rumble of power shook the vault.

'What was that?' asked Engin apprehensively.

'The Master at work, I should imagine. Now come on, Spandrell, there's no time to waste.'

It didn't take the Master long to remember that he had come, not to admire the Eye of Harmony, but to steal it. Settling the gleaming Sash of Rassilon about his shoulders, to protect him from the monolith's energy-field, he began uncoupling the first of the six coils. As he freed the link and withdrew it, there was a deep ominous rumbling from the chasm below the monolith. Already the energy-balance had been disturbed.

Back against one wall, legs against the other, the Doctor edged his way slowly up the smooth metal shaft. He seemed to have been climbing forever. He paused to rest, and great drops of sweat splashed from his forehead and trickled down his nose. Far below he could just see the faces of Spandrell and Engin, peering anxiously up the shaft. Above was only the tiny gleam of light that never seemed to get any nearer. The whole Panopticon was rumbling and shaking now, and so was the Doctor's shaft. Legs and back aching, eyes blinded with sweat, the Doctor continued his climb.

Working his way round the monolith, the Master was disconnecting one energy coil after another. As the imbalance of forces grew steadily greater, the rumbling from the chasm grew louder. The monolith itself began to hum with energy ... An earthquake-like tremor rocked the Panopticon, and an ominous crack appeared in the rear wall ...

The tremor almost shook the Doctor out of his shaft. He did actually slip back a few feet, then managed to brace himself again, thrusting legs and back against the vibrating sides of the shaft. The shaking lessened and he resumed his agonising climb.

Spandrell pulled Engin out of the way as a chunk of masonry crashed down from the ceiling. The whole vault was shaking. Engin looked at Spandrell in alarm. 'What is it? What's happening?'

'If the Doctor's right,' said Spandrell grimly, 'it's the beginning of the end of the world ...'

The Doctor was nearly at the top now. The shaft ended in a metal grille. Bracing himself awkwardly he kicked upwards with his right foot until the grille came free. The Doctor struggled through the gap and found he'd emerged through the floor of one of the Panopticon's outer corridors. The whole building was rumbling and shaking, and seemed about to fall on his head at any moment. Piercing through all the noise was a high-pitched whine of pure energy. The Doctor began running towards the sound.

Only two of the energy coils were connected now, and a storm of pure energy coming from the monolith was fast wrecking not only the Panopticon but most of the city around it. From outside the Panopticon came screams of terror and the crash of falling masonry.

The Master laughed. He paused to rest for a moment, clinging to the vibrating monolith. The effect of the contact with the energy-source was immediate and extraordinary. His limbs grew strong again, his back straightened. When he spoke, his voice had its old resonance. 'Rassilon's discovery,' he roared. 'All mine!' He hugged the monolith exultantly. 'When I bear this back to my TARDIS, it will give me supreme power over the Universe. I shall be Master of all matter!'

Moving quickly and confidently now, he bent to remove another coil. The coil came free, there was a sound like breaking ice and big cracks appeared in the Panopticon floor ...

As the Doctor ran into the hall a huge section of floor simply vanished before his feet, crashing away into nothingness. Jumping back, the Doctor skirted his way round the chasm and ran across the rapidly-crumbling floor. He arrived on the central dais, just as the Master bent to uncouple the final coil. 'Stop!' he shouted.

The Master looked up from his task. He seemed almost pleased to see the Doctor. 'Congratulations! You are just in time for the end!'

He began to uncouple the last energy coil.

'Don't!' shouted the Doctor. 'Unscrew that and you'll die as surely as any of us.'

The Master smiled and shook his head. 'You can do better than that, Doctor. I am wearing the Sash of Rassilon.' He touched the gleaming band of metal across his chest.

'So was the President when he was shot down. The

staser-bolt damaged the Sash. It won't protect you now—it's useless! Look!' and the Doctor pointed.

'You lie,' screamed the Master, but for a second he glanced down. In that second the Doctor hurled himself across the dais in an incredible flying tackle. They went down together in a tangle of arms and legs, rolling across the shuddering floor.

Despairingly the Doctor realised how much contact with the Eye of Harmony had restored the Master's strength. The scrawny limbs beneath his grip felt like coiled steel. With a savage heave the Master threw the Doctor from him, and bent to complete the uncoupling of the last energy-coil. As his hands closed on the connection, the Doctor scrabbled desperately across the floor and dragged him away. He pulled the Master to his feet and they grappled fiercely for a moment. Once again, the Master's new-found strength came to his aid. He flung the Doctor aside almost with ease, sprang back towards the monolith—and stumbled on a chunk of loose rubble. His foot twisted and he fell helplessly backwards. Arms flailing he pitched clear off the dais—and into the spreading chasm in the Panopticon floor ... For a moment the Master clutched desperately at the edge of the chasm, hanging on by two claw-like hands. Then the masonry crumbled away beneath his grip, and he fell screaming to the depths below.

The Doctor picked himself up, and began re-coupling energy-coils with frantic speed. As one coil after another was linked back into place, the subterranean rumbling steadied, diminished, and gradually died away ... Gallifrey had been saved.

12

An End—and a Beginning

The Chancellery office had lost much of its former
opulence. Half the roof had fallen in and there was
dust and rubble everywhere.

With a gesture of irritation, Cardinal Borusa swept
some chunks of loose masonry from his desk. 'Half
the city in ruins, untold damage. Countless lives
lost...'

Engin nodded sympathetically. 'Quite so, Cardinal.
Had it not been for the Doctor, it could have been
much worse.'

'Yes, indeed, I am quite conscious of the debt we
owe.' Borusa glanced a little awkwardly at the Doctor
who had recovered his own clothes from the museum
case, and was happily winding his incredibly long
scarf around his neck.

'Nevertheless,' Borusa continued gloomily. 'This is
still the greatest catastrophe Gallifrey has ever known.
What will we tell the people? What can we *say*?'

The Doctor rose, tilting his hat to a jaunty angle.
'You'll just have to adjust the truth again, Cardinal.
How about, oh I don't know ... Subsidence owing to
a plague of very large mice?'

Worn and harried as he was, Borusa still wasn't going to tolerate cheek from his old pupil. 'I believe I

told you long ago, Doctor, you will never amount to anything in the galaxy while you retain your propensity for vulgar facetiousness.'

For a moment the Doctor was back in the Academy again—then he grinned unabashed. 'Yes, sir, you did tell me that. Many times! Can I go now, sir?'

'Indeed you can, Doctor—preferably with the utmost despatch. Perhaps you will see that the transduction barriers are raised, Castellan?'

Spandrell had been watching them both with some apprehension. 'Of course, sir.' A little hurriedly, he ushered the Doctor towards the door.

As they reached it, Borusa called, 'Oh, Doctor?'

The Doctor turned. 'Yes, sir?'

There was the ghost of a smile on the Cardinal's face—he might almost have been feeling proud of his old pupil. 'Nine out of ten, Doctor.'

The Doctor smiled. 'Thank you, sir,' he said respectfully, and left.

Key in hand, the Doctor stood outside the TARDIS. Spandrell and Engin beside him. 'You know, Doctor, if you *wanted* to stay,' said Engin wistfully, 'I'm sure any past difficulties could be overlooked.'

The Doctor looked affectionately down at the old Co-ordinator. How could he make the old Time Lord understand ... 'No, I don't think I will, thanks all the same. Believe it or not, I actually like it out there.' He turned to the Castellan. 'Thank you, Spandrell— for trusting me.'

'It's we who should thank you, Doctor. You destroyed the Master.'

'I didn't actually *see* him die, you know. I was rather busy.'

Engin shuddered. 'But even if he did survive the fall—wasn't he dying anyway?'

The Doctor stared abstractedly at an ornate grandfather clock which stood near the TARDIS. 'There was a lot of energy coming from that monolith. The Sash of Rassilon might have enabled him to convert it.'

'You're not suggesting he's still alive?' asked Spandrell incredulously.

'I hope not. And there's no one else in all the galaxies I'd say that about. He's the quintessence of evil.' The Doctor had always hated farewells. Abruptly he said, 'Well, goodbye to you both,' and disappeared inside the TARDIS.

Spandrell and Engin stepped back as the TARDIS dematerialisation noise began. Seconds later the TARDIS had faded away.

They were about to go when they heard *another dematerialisation noise*. It seemed to be coming from the grandfather clock. For a moment the clock-face turned into a familiar skull-like face, lips curled in a mocking smile.

'Look,' shouted Spandrell. 'It's the Master!' He drew his staser-pistol but the clock had vanished.

Spandrell sighed, and holstered the staser. 'Too late —they've gone.'

Engin was considerably put out at this further

upset. '*Where* have they gone?' he demanded peevishly. 'Where do you think they're heading?'

Spandrell gestured expansively. 'Out into the Universe, Co-ordinator. And you know—I've a feeling it isn't big enough for both of them!'

SCIENCE FICTION

	0426200500	Terrance Dicks STAR QUEST: SPACEJACK	60p
	0426200748	Terrance Dicks STAR QUEST: ROBOWORLD	75p

'Doctor Who'

Δ	0426114558	Terrance Dicks DOCTOR WHO AND THE ABOMINABLE SNOWMEN	70p
Δ	0426200373	DOCTOR WHO AND THE ANDROID INVASION	75p
Δ	0426116313	Ian Marter DOCTOR WHO AND THE ARK IN SPACE	70p
Δ	0426112954	Terrance Dicks DOCTOR WHO AND THE AUTON INVASION	75p
Δ	0426116747	DOCTOR WHO AND THE BRAIN OF MORBIUS	75p
Δ	0426110250	DOCTOR WHO AND THE CARNIVAL OF MONSTERS	70p
Δ	042611471X	Malcolm Hulke DOCTOR WHO AND THE CAVE-MONSTERS	70p
Δ	0426117034	Terrance Dicks DOCTOR WHO AND THE CLAWS OF AXOS	75p
Δ	0426113160	David Whitaker DOCTOR WHO AND THE CRUSADERS	70p
Δ	0426114981	Brian Hayles DOCTOR WHO AND THE CURSE OF PELADON	70p
Δ	0426114639	Gerry Davis DOCTOR WHO AND THE CYBERMEN	70p
Δ	0426113322	Terrance Dicks DOCTOR WHO AND THE DAEMONS	75p
Δ	042611244X	DOCTOR WHO AND THE DALEK INVASION OF EARTH	70p
Δ	0426103807	DOCTOR WHO AND THE DAY OF THE DALEKS	70p
Δ	0426101103	David Whitaker DOCTOR WHO AND THE DALEKS	70p
Δ	0426119657	Terrance Dicks DOCTOR WHO AND THE DEADLY ASSASSIN	60p
Δ	042620042X	DOCTOR WHO – DEATH TO THE DALEKS	75p
Δ	0426200969	DOCTOR WHO AND THE DESTINY OF THE DALEKS	75p
Δ	0426108744	Malcolm Hulke DOCTOR WHO AND THE DINOSAUR INVASION	75p
Δ	0426103726	DOCTOR WHO AND THE DOOMSDAY WEAPON	70p

SCIENCE FICTION

Δ	0426200063	Terrance Dicks DOCTOR WHO AND THE FACE OF EVIL	70p
Δ	0426112601	DOCTOR WHO AND THE GENESIS OF THE DALEKS	75p
Δ	0426200330	DOCTOR WHO AND THE HAND OF FEAR	75p
Δ	0426200098	DOCTOR WHO AND THE HORROR OF FANG ROCK	70p
Δ	0426108663	Brian Hayles DOCTOR WHO AND THE ICE WARRIORS	70p
Δ	0426200772	Terrance Dicks DOCTOR WHO AND THE IMAGE OF THE FENDAHL	70p
Δ	0426200934	DOCTOR WHO AND THE INVASION OF TIME	75p
Δ	0426200543	DOCTOR WHO AND THE INVISIBLE ENEMY	75p
Δ	0426118936	Philip Hinchcliffe DOCTOR WHO AND THE MASQUE OF MANDRAGORA	70p
Δ	0426116909	Terrance Dicks DOCTOR WHO AND THE MUTANTS	75p
Δ	0426116828	DOCTOR WHO AND THE PLANET OF EVIL	75p
Δ	0426116666	DOCTOR WHO AND THE PYRAMIDS OF MARS	75p
Δ	042610997X	DOCTOR WHO AND THE REVENGE OF THE CYBERMAN	75p
Δ	0426200926	Ian Marter DOCTOR WHO AND THE RIBOS OPERATION	75p
Δ	0426200616	Terrance Dicks DOCTOR WHO AND THE ROBOTS OF DEATH	70p
Δ	042611308X	Malcolm Hulke DOCTOR WHO AND THE SEA-DEVILS	70p
Δ	0426116585	Philip Hinchcliffe DOCTOR WHO AND THE SEEDS OF DOOM	60p
Δ	0426200497	Ian Marter DOCTOR WHO AND THE SONTARAN EXPERIMENT	60p
Δ	0426200993	Terrance Dicks DOCTOR WHO AND THE STONES OF BLOOD	75p
Δ	0426110684	Gerry Davis DOCTOR WHO AND THE TENTH PLANET	75p
Δ	0426119738	Terrance Dicks DOCTOR WHO AND THE TALONS OF WENG CHIANG	75p

† For sale in Britain and Ireland only.
* Not for sale in Canada. • Reissues.
Δ Film & T.V. tie-ins

SCIENCE FICTION

	'0426118421	DOCTOR WHO DINOSAUR BOOK (illus)	75p
	0426200020	DOCTOR WHO DISCOVERS PREHISTORIC ANIMALS (NF) (illus)	75p
	0426200039	DOCTOR WHO DISCOVERS SPACE TRAVEL (NF) (illus)	75p
	0426200047	DOCTOR WHO DISCOVERS STRANGE AND MYSTERIOUS CREATURES (NF) (illus)	75p
	042620008X	DOCTOR WHO DISCOVERS THE STORY OF EARLY MAN (NF) (illus)	75p
	0426200136	DOCTOR WHO DISCOVERS THE CONQUERORS (NF) (illus)	75p
Δ	0426200640	Terrance Dicks JUNIOR DR WHO: THE GIANT ROBOT (illus)	75p
Δ	0426115783	DOCTOR WHO AND THE THREE DOCTORS	75p
Δ	0426200233	DOCTOR WHO AND THE TIME WARRIOR	75p
Δ	0426110765	Gerry Davis DOCTOR WHO AND THE TOMB OF THE CYBERMEN	75p
Δ	0426200683	Terrance Dicks DOCTOR WHO AND THE UNDERWORLD	75p
Δ	0426200829	Malcolm Hulke DOCTOR WHO AND THE WAR GAMES	75p
Δ	0426110846	Terrance Dicks DOCTOR WHO AND THE WEB OF FEAR	75p
Δ	0426113241	Bill Strutton DOCTOR WHO AND THE ZARBI (illus)	70p
Δ	0426200675	Terrance Dicks THE ADVENTURES OF K9 AND OTHER MECHANICAL CREATURES (illus)	75p
Δ	0426200950	Terry Nation's DALEK SPECIAL (illus)	95p
Δ	0426114477	DOCTOR WHO MONSTER BOOK (Colour illus)	50p
Δ	0426200012	THE SECOND DOCTOR WHO MONSTER BOOK (Colour illus)	70p

† For sale in Britain and Ireland only.
* Not for sale in Canada. • Reissues.
Δ Film & T.V. tie-ins.

CHILDREN'S BOOKS

	Hilary Seton	
0426106989	**THE HUMBLES** (illus)	50p
	Jack Stoneley	
0426200381	**THE TUESDAY DOG** (illus)	60p
	Joyce Stranger	
042611017X	**THE SECRET HERDS** (illus)	45p
	Noel Streatfeild	
0426109112	**THE NOEL STREATFEILD CHRISTMAS HOLIDAY BOOK** (illus)	60p
0426109031	**THE NOEL STREATFEILD EASTER HOLIDAY BOOK** (illus)	60p
0426105249	**THE NOEL STREATFEILD SUMMER HOLIDAY BOOK** (illus)	50p
	Barbara Euphan Todd	
0426200152	**DETECTIVE WORZEL GUMMIDGE** (illus)	60p
0426200756	**WORZEL GUMMIDGE AND THE RAILWAY SCARECROWS** (illus)	60p

GENERAL NON-FICTION

	J. H. Elliott	
0426101456	**FISHING** (illus)	60p
	Plantagenet Somerset Fry	
0426200314	**BOUDICCA** (illus)	60p
	Elizabeth Gundrey	
0426108906	**THE SUMMER BOOK** (illus)	45p
	Larry Kettelkamp	
0426113594	**INVESTIGATING UFOs** (illus)	50p*
	G. J. B. Laverty	
0426118340	**THE TARGET BOOK OF CROSSWORDS FOR FUN**	50p
	Carey Miller	
0426114396	**THE TARGET BOOK OF FATE AND FORTUNE** (illus)	50p
	D. & C. Power	
0426117115	**THE TARGET BOOK OF PICTURE PUZZLES** (illus)	40p
	Christopher Reynolds	
042610823X	**CREATURES OF THE BAY** (illus)	50p
	E. Schlossberg and J. Brockman	
0426200608	**THE KIDS' POCKET CALCULATOR GAME BOOK** (illus)	60p*
	David Shaw	
0426112369	**CRAFTS FOR GIRLS** (illus)	50p
042610532X	**THE 2nd TARGET BOOK OF FUN AND GAMES** (illus)	30p
0426109465	**THE 3rd TARGET BOOK OF FUN AND GAMES** (illus)	50p
	R. W. Wilson	
0426104366	**THE LONDON QUIZ BOOK** (illus)	60p

† For sale in Britain and Ireland only.
* Not for sale in Canada. ● Reissues.
Δ Film & T.V. tie-ins.

If you enjoyed this book and would like to have information sent to you about other TARGET titles, write to the address below.

You will also receive:
A FREE TARGET BADGE!
Based on the TARGET BOOKS symbol — see front cover of this book — this attractive three-colour badge, pinned to your blazer-lapel or jumper, will excite the interest and comment of all your friends!

and you will be further entitled to:
FREE ENTRY INTO THE TARGET DRAW!
All you have to do is cut off the coupon below, write on it your name and address in *block capitals,* and pin it to your letter. Twice a year, in June, and December, coupons will be drawn 'from the hat' and the winner will receive a complete year's set of TARGET books.

Write to:

TARGET BOOKS
44 Hill Street
London W1X 8LB

cut here

Full name ....

Address...

....

....

Age......................

PLEASE ENCLOSE A SELF-ADDRESSED STAMPED ENVELOPE WITH YOUR COUPON!

The

NOTEBOOKS OF
MALTE LAURIDS BRIGGE

Rainer Maria Rilke

➤➤❮❮

The

NOTEBOOKS OF
MALTE LAURIDS
BRIGGE

➤➤❮❮

Translated by
M. D. HERTER NORTON

CAPRICORN BOOKS   NEW YORK

Reprinted by arrangement with W. W. Norton & Company, Inc.
Capricorn Books, G. P. Putnam's Sons, New York
1958

Translated from the German:
Die Aufzeichnungen des Malte Laurids Brigge

Library of Congress Catalog
Card Number: 58-59757

MANUFACTURED IN THE UNITED STATES OF AMERICA

CONTENTS

➤➤➤ ◄◄◄